RUBY
ELECTRIC

RUBY ELECTRIC

A NOVEL BY
THERESA NELSON

SIMON &
SCHUSTER

Simon & Schuster
London

SIMON &
SCHUSTER

First published in Great Britain by Simon & Schuster UK Ltd, 2003
A Viacom company

First published in 2003 by Atheneum Books for Young Readers,
an imprint of Simon & Schuster Children's Division, New York.
Copyright © Theresa Nelson, 2003

1 3 5 7 9 10 8 6 4 2

Simon & Schuster UK Ltd
Africa House
64-78 Kingsway
London WC2B 6AH

A CIP catalogue record for this book is available from the British Library

ISBN 0689837585

Typeset by SX Composing DTP, Rayleigh, Essex
Printed and bound in Great Britain by
Bookmarque Ltd, Croydon, surrey

For Richard Jackson – the one and only DJ –
and his dear wife, Nancy,
and for their grandchildren, Kelsey and Alexander Albert

Rat-a-tat
Pow! Pow! Pow!
Rat-a-tat

FADE IN:

The Vanishing Point, it's called. "The Little Café with the Big Screen Flavour." It might seem familiar. There's a fake Hollywood restaurant for every mini-mall in the San Fernando Valley.

This one's right next door to Pagliacci's Rent-a-Clown, all but hidden behind their Bozo banner. A person could pass by and never even know it.

That's what has Ruby worried.

Her mother gives her a look. "You okay, honey?"

Ruby stares at her chopsticks. "Sure."

She sinks back in the bamboo seat.

Closes her eyes.

THE SCREEN GOES BLACK

At first you can hardly hear the tapping. It's only the ghost of a sound. Away off in the dark somewhere, a distant drumming, gradually growing louder:

Rat-a-tat
POW! POW! POW!

FADE IN . . . slowly . . .

Now you can see it, too. A single hand, sending out Morse code on an old-time telegraph machine:

POW! POW! POW!
Rat-a-tat
Rat-a-tat

Now the camera PULLS BACK, showing more of the picture. The hand belongs to a girl. A beautiful girl. A beautiful, blue-eyed, golden-haired girl. No freckles. Quite tall for twelve. (You can tell this right away, even though she's hunched over the machine, tapping with all her might.)

TALL GIRL
SOS! SOS! Come in! Come in!
Don't you hear me? SOS! SOS!
Somebody, anybody, please!

CUT TO a long shot of a ship in distress.

Lights flickering, people shrieking, icy water pouring
through the portholes.

MOVE IN CLOSER: On the deck (tilted now at a
sickening angle) the lifeboats are being lowered.
But not enough. Not nearly enough. Any fool can
see that. As frantic passengers claw their way
towards them, and crew members struggle to keep
order, a band of brave musicians plays a lilting
melody:

> Yankee Doodle went to town,
> Just to ride a pony,
> Stuck a feather in his cap
> And called it maca –

"Ruby!"

Still the tireless TALL GIRL in the telegraph office
pounds out her tortured message:

> SOS! SOS!
> Come in, please!
> Rat-a-tat –

"Ruby!"
The ship disappears. The band stops playing. The
chopsticks rap out a sharp staccato on the edge of the
café table.

POW!
Rat-a-tat
Rat-a-

Pearl Miller reaches across a plate of egg rolls and touches her daughter's wrist. The chopsticks freeze in mid-air.

"Thank you," says Pearl. "Have an egg roll."

"No, thanks."

"Come on. Just one. They're delicious."

Ruby shakes her head. It's a very red head. She squints behind her glasses, trying to change the picture again . . .

No use. She's still wedged in a half-size corner booth by the window with her mother and her little brother, Pete, still sitting there staring at the pair of them across the soy sauce.

"Not much longer," Mama says. "Another five minutes, maybe. We'll give him another five minutes."

Mama and Pete are both red-headed too, but otherwise normal-looking. Even somewhat better than normal, in Mama's case. She was almost a beauty queen once. In her younger days back in Texas, she was fourth runner-up for Miss Wichita Falls. Of course she would tell you that's all ancient history; it kind of embarrasses her now. But sometimes Ruby gets chills just thinking how a simple twist of fate might have altered their entire lives. What if the actual winner had been unexpectedly visited by some hideous disfigurement? Attacked by marauding bears, say, during a fun-filled but ultimately tragic vacation in Yellowstone? Would they be sitting here right now if, for any reason, the first, second, and third runners-up had been unable to fulfil their duties?

Ice cubes clink. A fat man laughs. A guy with a beard drops his napkin.

As for Pete – well, Pete is Pete, that's all. Freckles are fine when you're six.

Ruby, on the other hand, has been twelve and a half all year.

"You're sure you're not hungry? You're both bound to be tired. Maybe we ought to –"

"I'm *okay*, Mum." Ruby's fists (square-shaped, freckles on the otherwise white knuckles) clench around the chopsticks. "We're okay, right, Pete?"

"Pete's gone," says Pete. He holds up a ragged woolly mammoth puppet. "I am authorised to take all messages."

"Give me a break."

"My name is Mammook."

"Just another five minutes," says Mama.

Ruby looks out of the window. Not much there, really. Just a pigeon pecking at a bug on the ledge and the traffic crawling by on Ventura Boulevard and the summer sun setting in a smoggy haze behind the Sizzler across the street. Still, from where Ruby sits, she has a clear view of the pavement, so she'll be the first to see him, if he comes.

Frankie Miller, that is.

Her father.

When he comes, that is.

Rat-a-tat
POW! POW! POW!
Rat-a-tat

The ship is sinking fast now. Salt water floods the telegraph office. Still, the TALL GIRL refuses to relinquish her post, though she's up to her waist in the stinking brine:

SOS! SOS!
Rat-a-tat
POW! POW! PO –

Pete gives Ruby a nudge in the rubs. "You're doing it again," he whispers.

"Shut up, Mammook." She pokes him with a chopstick.

Their mother signals the waitress. "The bill, please."

"No! He's coming. He promised."

"It's almost eight o'clock, Ruby. We've been here an hour and a half."

"Well, maybe he got lost."

"Oh, honey –"

"Maybe he got tied up in traffic or there was an accident or –"

"Are you finished, miss?" asks the waitress, leaning in to take away the egg rolls.

"Yes . . . I mean, no!" Ruby grabs the plate, playing tug of war until she wins, spilling half a bowl of fried rice in Pete's lap. "I'm still eating, okay,

Mum? I'm hungry now. See? You're right, these are really good."

Mama sighs. She nods at the waitress, who walks away with a shrug.

"Five minutes. Tops." Mama shows her watch to Ruby. "Then we're leaving. Got it?"

"Got it," says Ruby, her mouth full of stone-cold shrimp, her eyes on the little black second hand, ticking away.

Rat-a-tat
POW! POW! POW!
Rat-a-tat

CUT TO a second ship, far from the first. Below deck, a YOUNG NAVAL OFFICER is receiving a telegraph signal.

YOUNG OFFICER
SOS. SOS? Dear God, not the "Titanic"?!

He rips the printed page from his telegraph machine and tears out of the office.

CUT TO the ship's bow. The CAPTAIN stands at the rail. Square-jawed. Intrepid. A glint of granite in his keen blue eyes. Clearly a man among men. As he gazes out on the moonlit waves, the YOUNG OFFICER comes running.

YOUNG OFFICER

SOS, sir. From the "Titanic". It's just come in.

CAPTAIN

Well, what are we waiting for, Lieutenant?
Turn the ship around!

YOUNG OFFICER

Yes, sir. Right away, sir. But –

CAPTAIN

But what? Speak up, Lieutenant! We've no time
to waste!

YOUNG OFFICER

But . . . well, sir . . the radar doesn't seem to be
working properly, and unless we can re-wire
the throckmorton and decode the coleanthus,
I'm afraid that –

CAPTAIN

Confound it, man, speak plainly!

YOUNG OFFICER

I'm not sure we can find them, sir.

A blue minivan pulls into the Sizzler car park. An
enormous family climbs out. Six or seven kids and a
worn-out-looking mother. Last of all comes the father,
talking on his mobile. Trailing after the others, taking

his time. He's still deep in conversation when the littlest kid (a tiny girl in a ridiculous pink tutu) turns around and comes skipping back to him. She pulls on his shirt sleeve. He doesn't notice her. She pulls again. Now he looks down and sees her looking up at him, waiting. Ruby figures he'll get mad, but he doesn't seem mad. He smiles and touches the kid's wild curls and finishes his call. Then he hoists her up on his shoulder and carries her inside.

POW! POW! POW!

On the doomed ship, the last dim light begins to die. The end is near, but the TALL GIRL isn't crying. You might think she is, but you're wrong, okay? She grits her teeth. She's no cry-baby.

SOS! SOS!

Why didn't we go to the Sizzler? All you can eat and a sign as big as Dallas.

"Ruby? It's time."

SOS! SOS!

Anybody can find the Sizzler . . .

"We're waiting, Ruby. Don't you hear me?"

Don't you hear me?

SOS

Rat-a-tat

Pow.

2

Okay, so he didn't show up again. There's probably a perfectly logical explanation. Ruby can think of twenty or thirty reasons, without half trying.

When you're Frankie Miller's daughter, you have to read between the lines, that's all. Oh sure, no one has actually come out and said it – well, how could they, when it might be a question of national security? – but the more Ruby thinks about it, the more certain she is that the CIA is involved. The clues are all there, if you're paying attention – not just her dad's calling out of the blue again last night and then failing to appear like always, but the whole thing: his sudden disappearance from their lives five years ago, their mother's crazy decision to move to LA, her flimsy attempts to cover the fact that she's hiding something.

Like the day Daddy left. And what's Mama doing? Sitting on the rug in the TV room, cutting out paper dolls. That's what Ruby *thought* she was doing, anyhow, making paper dolls and watching some old film on the video, while Pete sucked his thumb and Ruby played dressing-up, clomping around the house in Mama's high-heeled shoes.

They were beautiful, those shoes – beautiful black patent leather, except for the scuff marks on the back. Look, Mama, said Ruby, showing her the ugly white patches, but Mama said not to worry; they could cover those up later with Magic Marker. Her eyes were all red for some reason, and there were tears slipping out the corners and sliding down her face, sliding down, down, all the way to her chin, leaving shining trails like the ones snails left on the pavements in summer.

Magic Marker? Ruby repeated. She didn't understand why her mother was crying. It wasn't a sad film. It was *Groundhog Day*, for heaven's sake – the one where the dumb guy keeps waking up on the same morning and has to live it over and over, till he gets it right. It was Daddy's all-time favourite comedy. The whole family had watched it just the other night and laughed like loons. So why wasn't Mama laughing now? Ruby wondered.

Magic Marker? she said again, touching a tear track with her pointing finger. Yes, baby, said Mama, catching hold of Ruby's hand and covering it with kisses. No one will ever know the difference. And she hugged Ruby so hard it hurt, and Ruby looked down at her scuffed-up shoes, and then she remembered the paper dolls and worried about stepping on them. But there weren't any paper dolls there. Just a pile of empty picture frames and a trillion pieces of Daddy, scattered all over the old blue rug.

"Who wants ice cream?" their mother asks, as they climb in the car outside the Vanishing Point.

"No, thanks," says Ruby. She can't be bought that cheaply, not while their father is still out there somewhere, probably dodging an assassin's bullets or making an emergency landing in the president's private plane or —

"Can I have chocolate chip?" says Pete.

Ruby gives him her most disdainful look. She hopes so, anyway. She's not positive she's ever actually seen this type of look, but she read about one last week in a book called *The Whispering Heart* and has been eagerly awaiting an opportunity to try out her version on somebody. Like the heroine (Lady Lydia Tyrone), she lifts her finely sculpted chin one notch higher.

Pete, however, ignores her. She in turn is forced to ignore his cheerful slurping as they drive home in their '89 Ford, also known as the Purple Demon, while she stares out of the rear window in stony silence. (That was in the book too. *How can silence be stony?* she wondered at the time, but she understands now: silent as a stone. A tombstone, maybe. That's about the size of it — that's about how this feels — like somebody just died.)

Not that she can blame Pete, really. He had just turned two the last time they saw their father. He wouldn't know him from Adam. Even Ruby has trouble sometimes, making his face come clear. All she's got to go on now is one crummy little snapshot, and you can hardly see him in that. Which is probably the one thing that saved it when Mama went nuts with the scissors.

Ruby slips it out of her wallet now, while nobody's paying attention. She studies the picture for the millionth time. It doesn't *seem* all that mysterious – at least, on the surface. But maybe she just needs stronger lenses . . .

It was taken at some park, on her own sixth birthday. There are balloons and a cake and a bunch of little kids in paper hats sitting at a picnic table under a scrawny tree. Ruby is right in the middle, looking even homelier than usual. She's got chocolate all around her mouth, and a big dopey grin, and both her front teeth are missing. (You'd think somebody could have reminded her, as a personal favour.) Mama must have been taking the picture; it looks like she was having her same old trouble with the light meter. Half the kids are squinting themselves pea-eyed in the sunshine, and the other half – the ones in the shade – are all but invisible.

But if you look really hard in the shady part, half-hidden behind a Daisy Duck balloon, you can just make out Ruby's dad, standing there smiling, with his hand on her shoulder. You can make out his teeth, anyway. Unlike Ruby's, they appear to be all there. If you look even harder, though, you can tell that the two in the middle are a little brighter than the others. This is because they're fake, due to the real ones getting busted with a beer bottle by some dumb punk kid

Daddy was trying to arrest for being drunk and disorderly.

He isn't wearing his uniform in the picture. If Ruby were putting this in a film, she'd have him wearing it, of course, so you'd know right away that he was a policeman. This is called exposition, which is all the junk in the first part of the film that helps you figure out who everybody is and how they come into the story. Ruby doesn't care much for exposition, because it is no end of trouble, plus from what she's seen, half the audience is still too busy with their popcorn to pay attention anyhow. But as a future professional, she can't afford to skip steps. Turns out there are *rules* about this stuff. They have a whole stack of books on it over at the library; Ruby plans to read every one of them, just to be safe. So far she's checked out *Cut to the Chase: From Brainstorm to Blockbuster in Thirty Days* and *It's a Sled, Stupid: Unravelling the Mystery Behind the Making of Citizen* —

"Uh-oh," says Pete.

Ruby slips the picture back in her wallet and looks up, expecting a chocolate chip disaster. But they're almost home free; Mama is turning on to their street, and Pete still hasn't spilled a drop. And then Ruby sees where he's looking.

A police car is stopped in the driveway of their apartment block.

For a second she can't breathe. *I knew it. I knew he'd come . . .*

But it's not Frankie Miller's car. It doesn't even have

Texas plates; the seal on the side says "City of Los Angeles". And there's some officer Ruby's never laid eyes on, standing on the front porch, talking to their landlady, Miss Angela Pierce.

3

"*Now* what?" Their mother sighs and switches off the engine. "She doesn't look happy, does she?"

It's true. Miss Pierce doesn't look one bit happy. Not that she's ever been exactly a barrel of laughs. She reminds Ruby of Almira Gulch in *The Wizard of Oz* — the old maid who's always so crabby about Toto bothering her cat. Only Miss Pierce is even older — eighty, at least — and she's not too fond of cats, either. This is because they tend to chase Lord Byron, her nightmare of a parrot, who is up there sitting on her shoulder this very minute, squawking along with her at the poor policeman.

"Maybe we should come back later," Ruby suggests.

But Mama sighs again and shakes her head. "We'd better go see what's up."

It could be worse, Ruby supposes. Half the time Miss Pierce lets the stupid bird ride around on her head. ("He's as well trained as you are" was her frosty answer when Pete first asked the obvious question.) Still, the overall weirdness of the whole parrot deal is plenty embarrassing. What if the officer should think they're somehow *related* to the bird lady? Good Lord. "We could just cruise around the block until he's gone . . ."

But Pete and Mammook are already out of the car and halfway across the minuscule garden. He loves police shows – *Hawaii Five-0* reruns are his favourites – plus he's a sucker for late-breaking news. And Ruby gets a definite sinking feeling, from the way he's holding what's left of his ice-cream cone in front of the puppet, that he's pretending it's a microphone. *Please, dear God,* she prays, scrambling to follow, *don't let him ask the policeman for an interview.*

Fortunately, Miss Pierce is so wound up that Mammook couldn't get a word in even if he wanted to.

"But I can *identify* them, Officer, both of them, don't you understand? I could pick them out of a line-up with absolute certainty."

"Yes, ma'am, I'm sure you could, but I'm afraid without an address, there's not much we can –"

"I know they live in the neighbourhood; I'm positive it was the same two boys who nearly ran me down with their skateboards just last week."

"Yes, ma'am, but –"

"It's the tall one who's the ringleader, that's obvious. He was doing most of the damage. But the short one's no better. He *smiled* at me when he heard me calling – the most insolent little goblin grin you ever saw – and then he pointed me out to his friend, and that was when the two of them turned around and –"

Miss Pierce breaks off there, suddenly aware of her

audience – particularly Pete, leaning in with his cone-mike for the scoop. "Well, you know –" Miss Pierce lowers her voice. "Turned around and . . . as I said before."

The officer checks his notes. "Mooned you?" he finishes helpfully.

"Exactly," says Miss Pierce.

"SKKRRAAWK!" says Lord Byron. "Goodnight, moon, goodnight, moon, the moon lies fair upon the straits . . ."

"That will do, LB." There is a hint of pink in Miss Pierce's withered cheeks. She fixes Lord Byron with a look that shuts him up.

But a strangled sound comes from Mama, followed by a severe fit of coughing.

Miss Pierce raises an eyebrow. "Are you all right, Mrs Miller?"

"Yes . . . I'm sorry, I just . . . We just had ice cream . . . It must have . . . I'm fine, really."

The officer clears his throat. He turns back to Miss Pierce. "Well, I believe I have all I need here, ma'am, but if those kids should give you any more trouble –"

"Any *more* trouble? Haven't they done enough already?" Miss Pierce turns to Mama. "Just *look* at that ugly mess, Mrs Miller." She points a gnarled finger across the street. "Do you see? Do you see what those hooligans have done?" And then the finger begins to tremble. The sharp eyes fill with tears. "Do you see what they've done to the river?"

*

Maybe it's nuts to feel sorry for a geographical feature. Ruby isn't sure. But the Los Angeles River is a sorry-making sight, no question about it. For a good half-hour after the policeman leaves, and Mama and Pete take Miss Pierce inside for a cup of tea, Ruby sits on the porch steps, watching the water crawl by.

"It's just an old drainage ditch," she told her mother the first time she saw it, turning up her nose at its man-made banks. They had *real* rivers back in Texas. She ought to know; she had grown up right next to one. And this overblown cement gutter couldn't hold a candle to the Wichita.

But Mama defended it. It wasn't always like this, she said – all boxed in, like some wild animal in a cage. Used to be this river ran free as the wind, when the San Fernando Valley was nothing but country. Used to be it had nice soft sand on its bottom and sides, not these rock-hard prison walls. And fish, too – well, sure, but not just *fish*.

This river had a history. It was older than old. This river had woolly mammoths dropping by for a dip, once upon a time. Yes, ma'am, *mammoths*, Mama insisted, and when Ruby thought she was kidding, Mama took her and Pete to see their skeletons over at the La Brea Tar Pits. Like to have taken Pete's breath away, those monster bones, towering over him so. They had to buy Mammook in the gift shop just to calm him down. And there was more besides: dire wolves and giant sloths and condors, too – great dragon birds – with their wings spread so wide, a squirrel in their shadow at straight-up noon must have thought it was the end of the world.

It makes Ruby dizzy, even now, just thinking about this river in those days. Could be one of those old tigers with the sabre teeth came prowling right by here some sunny morning, twenty thousand years ago. Could be he bent over for a drink of these same waters, saw his own splendid savage self looking back. Could be he scared himself silly, that old cat. Could be he's running still . . .

And now look at it, Ruby thinks, casting her eyes on the crumpled crisp packet and crushed beer cans washing up on the concrete beach beneath the raw red scrawl of graffiti:

DEMUNS RUN BUT YOU CANOT HIDE

It makes her want to yell, that's what. It makes her want to punch somebody.

Two very specific somebodies, as a matter of fact.

MOVE IN CLOSE on the crisp packet . . .

It rises and falls in the shallow green waves. The current toys with it for a while, then catches it up and carries it out of Ruby's sight. It snags briefly on the half-submerged wheels of an upended shopping trolley, then breaks free and passes beneath an old metal service bridge –

Right under four dangling feet in battered trainers:

Sizes 13 and 5, respectively.

4

Big Skinny Bogart and his buddy Mouse are nowhere near 100 per cent guilty of half the stuff they get blamed for. Big Skinny has never scored 100 per cent on anything. Up until a particular morning this past May, he and Mouse were known chiefly for: (1) an inspired but unsuccessful attempt to put itching powder in the coach's jock strap, and (2) the remarkably lifelike quality of their armpit farts. But before that day, with these two modest exceptions, they were strictly below average, and proud of it.

The real trouble started all the way back in April, when the social studies teacher got the bright idea of setting joint research projects on assorted famous people, and then got the even *brighter* idea of teaming Big Skinny and Mouse with the smartest girl in school. That was actually fine with Big Skinny. He'd always secretly admired Ruby Miller. He couldn't get over somebody so little having such a big brain. But Mouse was kind of touchy about it. He claimed Miller was trying to get out of the whole deal, just because he *thought* he overheard her complaining to Mrs Haines about getting stuck with the year eight version of *Dumb and Dumber*.

"Aw, come on, Mouse, even if she did say it, we ought to take it as a compliment."

"Compliment?" Mouse looked sceptical. "How do you figure that?"

"Well, it was a pretty funny film, remember? She thinks we're funny, that's all."

"Yeah, right," said Mouse. He would never change his mind on that one. But even he had to admit there were certain advantages to being teamed with Miller. She'd probably want to do most of the work, for one thing. And as Big Skinny pointed out, since she'd never been known to get less than A minus, they might even end up with a good mark for once in their lives.

Sure enough, the research part was a breeze. For the next four weeks, Big Skinny and Mouse just goofed around on the library computer, mostly, and looked up their favourite dirty-sounding words in the online dictionary. (At last count, Lake Titicaca was still tops on their all-time hit list.) Meanwhile, Miller sat there scribbling like crazy in her notebook. Man, that girl could *write*. She would concentrate so hard her glasses would get all fogged up, and she wouldn't even notice it. Big Skinny offered to wipe them off for her once – she was such a little thing, sitting there working up a storm – but she looked at him like he was out of his mind, so he didn't bother her again.

And Mouse sort of tried to be friendly, in his way. He

did at least show her their *second*-favourite word, although Big Skinny was a little worried she might not appreciate that one: "asinine (as' ·nin), *adj.* [from the Latin *asininus*]: of an ass; also, like an ass, as in stupidity or obstinacy."

But she was a real good sport about it. "Perfect," she said. "Just perfect." And then she went right back to work.

Of course it was true she seemed a bit testy towards the end of the third week, when Big Skinny got around to asking her what she wanted him and Mouse to do on the actual day. She said to just *stand* there, for Pete's sake, and read the parts she'd written for them. They could do that much, couldn't they? And Mouse sort of took offence at that, because the truth was he sometimes had a little trouble with that kind of thing.

But he'd pretty much forgotten about it by the morning of their turn. In fact, he and Big Skinny had pretty much forgotten about the whole project, because just the night before, Mouse had come up with this great plan that was going to be the funniest thing that ever happened in the history of Rutherford B. Hayes Middle School . . .

"Okay. What's going on? What are you guys up to?" Miller asked when they came in the classroom door. Just thinking how hysterical this other deal was going to be had the two of them giggling already.

"Who? Us?" said Mouse, trying to act innocent, and of course that cracked them up even worse, and they busted out laughing again just as the bell rang.

Miller clearly wanted to kill them. "If you mess this up –"

"Mess what up?" Mouse's face went blank.

"Our *project*, for Pete's sake. In two minutes! Didn't you study your parts?"

"Oh, sure," said Big Skinny, "no problem." Even though the truth was he hadn't even looked at his. But he didn't want to make her feel bad or anything, and anyway all they had to do was read them, right?

Mrs Haines was in a good mood, at least. "Vincent Bogart?" she called out, smiling at Big Skinny. "Matthew Mossbach? Ruby Miller? Are you ready with your project?"

"Yes, ma'am," said Miller, looking daggers at the boys. Which unfortunately just made the whole thing funnier. But Big Skinny got hold of himself and poked Mouse in the ribs, and then they all took their places on the podium at the front.

Miller opened her notebook. Straightened those smudged-up glasses. Cleared her throat and took a deep breath. "As Arthur Wellesley, the great Duke of Wellington, once said of his own troops –"

Beside her, Big Skinny burped softly.

He didn't mean to. He really didn't. It was only nerves, was all. But it just about killed poor old Mouse. He doubled over in pain, his entire pint-size body shaking with strangled laughter, which of course set Big Skinny off again too.

"Is there a problem?" Mrs Haines asked.

"No problem," said Miller, glaring at her helpless

partners. She took an even *deeper* breath. "I don't know what effect these men will have on the enemy, but by God they terrify me."

Whoa. Big Skinny beamed with pride. Could that girl write or what? But before she could get another word out, Charlotte Burton's hand shot up.

Miller looked at the teacher.

"Is it important, Charlotte?" Mrs Haines asked.

"I have to be excused from the rest of this class if there's going to be cursing in it."

"Oh, please." Miller rolled her eyes. "I wasn't cursing, I was *quoting*."

"Well, that doesn't matter. It still counts."

"Now, Charlotte," said Mrs Haines, "there's really no need to take offence here."

"Cursing is cursing, that's all."

"Naw, man . . ." Big Skinny tried to help out a little. "She said, 'As the *Duke* said.' That makes it cool, get it? That's like when your mum wants to curse, she goes, 'As your *father* would say, you look like a tub of —'"

"Thank you, Vincent," said Mrs Haines. "I think we get your point."

But Big Skinny wasn't finished. "Anyway, you can't change the Duke. He always talks like that. We just seen him in — what was that old cowboy show we watched, Mouse?"

"The one where he wears that patch on his eye?"

"Naw, not *True Grit*, the other one. You remember: 'Take 'em to Missouri.'"

"Aw, yeah, *Red River*. The Duke was cool in that."

Miller's mouth dropped open. "Not John Wayne, you morons! Not *that* Duke!"

They looked at her in surprise. "Well, who then?" asked Big Skinny.

"The Duke of *Wellington*!" Ruby wailed. "The Duke of —"

"*EEEYYOOOO!*" Just then a colossal groan went up from the middle of the back row. Within seconds, the room was filled with the most putrid stench you ever even heard of and the sound of two dozen kids screeching and gagging at the same time.

"Stink bomb! Stink bomb!"

"Aw, *yuck*!"

"That is SO GROSS!"

"All right, everybody, you know the drill. Follow me. Don't panic. Let's just clear the room . . ."

Well, you couldn't help laughing at a thing like that, even if it wasn't exactly what they'd planned. Big Skinny couldn't anyway. But old Miller didn't seem to think it was all that funny. She didn't scream or yell like the others, though. She just shot Big Skinny and Mouse a couple of hundred more eyeball daggers. Cold as ice, every one. And then she ripped her speech out of her notebook and dropped it in the bin. "I'll get you for this."

Old Mouse, he was laughing too hard to answer, but Big Skinny managed to croak a "No, wait!" as he followed her out of the room. "It wasn't supposed to go off now . . . We didn't mean for . . . Come on, Miller, wait up!"

She turned around and looked at him. Big Skinny's heart stood still . . .

Coldly – oh, so coldly – she slammed the door in his face.

5

DEMUNS RUN BUT YOU CANOT HIDE . . .

It's them. Ruby knows it's them. How many other giggling hooligans spell like that?

She could have spoken up. She could still speak up. Maybe she will; maybe she'll get up off these porch steps and go find that nice policeman again and tell him their names right now. She could do it, no problem. She even knows the crummy apartments where they live. One snap of her fingers and they'll be behind bars where they belong.

So why is she still sitting here?

"It was only a joke!" Big Skinny kept saying that day, following her around even after she slammed the door on him. "The timing was just a little off, that's all. I swear, Miller, we didn't mean to mess up your speech . . ." He was still shouting as he and Mouse were being dragged away for judgement. "Do you hear what I'm saying, Miller? It was only a *jo-o-o-o-o-oke* . . ."

It had taken the head about five minutes to find out who was to blame, since the ghastly stink was coming directly from Mouse's backpack. (He had unwisely left it on the floor next to a heating vent, which – owing to an unseasonable dip in temperature – had been chugging out just enough hot air to set it off an hour ahead of schedule.) Big Skinny and he didn't try to lie about it or anything. They were mostly just upset that the thing hadn't gone off during assembly, like it was supposed to, in the middle of the head's annual lecture on good citizenship. Now, *that* would have been hilarious, in their opinion.

Unfortunately no one in the office – including the head himself – seemed to share this view, so Big Skinny and Mouse spent the rest of the school year in something called in-school suspension. Anybody else would have been kicked out altogether, but since *not* going to school wouldn't exactly be a punishment for this pair (more in the order of a dream come true), the PE teacher, "Wild Man" McCullough, said he'd be only too happy to keep them busy.

Not that Ruby gave a flip, of course. She was *glad* they were suffering. It was a *relief* not to have to put up with their stupid smirks. She was *delighted* to pass the detention hall on her way to class and see the two of them sitting there under the PE teacher's eagle eye, copying out the entire Constitution of the United States in their neatest handwriting. Good riddance, was what she thought.

But then . . .

One morning after social studies, Mrs Haines stopped her on her way out the door and handed her back her

Wellington speech, with an A plus in bright red ink on the front page.

Ruby looked at it in surprise. Mrs Haines had made it clear when she assigned the projects that the teams would be judged as a whole. All partners would get the same mark, no matter who did what. Not that Ruby was being pessimistic or anything, but considering how *their* presentation had gone, she was expecting a big fat zero. "I don't understand," she said.

Mrs Haines smiled. "Vincent dug it out of the bin. He said he was sorry about what happened. He said you did all the work, and it wasn't fair if you failed because of him."

Ruby was speechless. It was like getting a note of apology from Godzilla after he smashed your house and disintegrated your grandmother. What are you supposed to say to somebody like that? *Oh, okay, no sweat, she was past her prime anyhow?* Good grief. Now Ruby was confused. What was he trying to do – cheat her out of being able to hate him with a clear conscience?

Which is why she's still just sitting here, staring at those dumb red words on the river wall, when the door behind her opens, and Mama and Pete come back out on the porch with the old lady and her parrot.

"Any further sign of them?" Miss Pierce asks.

"No, ma'am," says Ruby. It's the truth, if not exactly the *whole* truth. All the same, the blood comes rushing to her face. Suddenly she has the uncomfortable feeling Miss Pierce can read minds. She's doing it right now, isn't she? Looking straight through Ruby's skull at the sputtering little cluster of synapses where Big Skinny and Mouse are peeking out, grinning.

But Miss Pierce just strokes Lord Byron's green feathers and says, "Hmmph. Well, keep your eyes peeled. And if you do notice anything out of the ordinary – anything at all – you'll let me know right away, won't you?"

"Yes, ma'am." *Sputter, sputter*. "Right away."

Miss Pierce studies her for a moment more, then turns to Mama. "Thank you again for the tea, Mrs Miller. I feel I can face anything now."

Mama shakes her hand. "It was our pleasure. Really."

"So we'll see you at the meeting?"

"I'll be there."

"Well, goodnight, then."

"Goodnight."

"SKKRRAAWK!" says Lord Byron. "Goodnight, goodnight, sweet prince . . ."

Pete laughs. Miss Pierce lifts an eyebrow. Then she gives him a wink. "And flights of angels sing thee to thy rest."

It's such a regal exit line that Ruby half expects a coachman to appear and whisk her away in the imperial carriage. But since Miss Pierce only lives a couple of feet away, in the other half of the building, all she does is open the door directly next to the Millers' and walk inside.

"What meeting?" Ruby asks her mother.

Before Mama can answer, the telephone starts ringing.

6

Ruby's heart gives a wild leap. *It's Daddy. He's calling to explain . . .*

"I'll get it!" she cries, pushing past the others and racing inside the grab the receiver. "Hello?"

"Hi, Ruby. It's Frieda. Is you mum home?"

Ruby sighs. "Just a minute." She hands the phone to her mother. Then she goes to her room and throws herself on her bed. Why are phone calls in real life always so *boring*? she wonders. When a person gets a call in a film, you know it's going to *matter*. Not once is it just a stupid wrong number, or somebody trying to sell something, or the Salvation Army asking if you have any used but still usable household items you'd like to donate to the poor. ("Did you tell them we *are* the poor?" Ruby asked her mother when this happened last week.) Or even worse, Frieda Hamley, the other receptionist at the South Central Valley Chiropody Centre, calling to ask if Mama can cover for her again because she's got to go to another audition for an antacid advert or take her dog to get its toenails clipped or whatever the latest emergency is.

"Monday morning?" Ruby can hear Mama saying. "Let's see now. Is that this Monday, the eighteenth?"

Oh, come on, Mama. Say no for a change. Just for kicks. Just once, to see how it feels.

"Well, sure, Frieda, I guess so . . . I don't think that should be a problem."

Like there was a snowball's chance in hell she might have actually said no.

It's not that Ruby is sorry her mother is a nice person. Nice is great. It's just not . . . *enough*. Nice just lies there like old lino, waiting for everybody to stomp their big number tens all over it. People like that Frieda, always taking advantage. It's not *fair*, that's all. She's already been on two local car dealers adverts and a national one for whipped topping, and she's not even half as pretty as Mama. It drives Ruby nuts. She knows her mother could make it big if she'd only try, but "I'm not the type," she always says. Like that's an excuse. Pearl Miller is probably the only almost ex-beauty queen in Los Angeles who *didn't* move out here to break into show business.

So why come, then?

"The Pacific Ocean. I'd always wanted to see it. And you'd never been to Disneyland, remember?"

Oh, yeah. The Disneyland scam. *That* was how she sucked them in.

At seven and two, some kids will believe anything.

"We're going to the Magic Kingdom," she kept telling them while she packed.

"Is Daddy coming?" Ruby asked.

"No."

"But —"

"*No.*" Mama wouldn't talk about him, even then. She did her best to change the subject. "Mickey will be there."

Pete's eyes lit up. "We're going to live with *Mickey?*"

All the way to California, he was convinced they were moving in with the actual mouse.

Ruby, being older and wiser, knew better. And of course once they got there, even Pete could see it was a trick. After one perfect day in the kingdom, home turned out to be a pink apartment-motel with a kitchenette — sticking-plaster pink — wedged in between the beer-making factory and the main highway.

"Flamingo Gardens," Mama read on the sign out front. "A garden flat! Won't that be nice?"

But Pete called it the Stinky Place and wrinkled his nose. "What's that cooking?" Ruby asked. "Green beans?"

"Not green beans. Hops. From the brewery," Mama explained.

Unfortunately that struck Pete as funny. "Beans hops!" he crowed, then proceeded to demonstrate, knocking over a lamp and smashing it to smithereens.

"You'll have to pay for that," said the manager. He'd been standing in the doorway, smoking a cigarette, while Mama and Ruby lugged the suitcases inside. There was a target-shaped gravy stain on the belly of his LA Lakers T-shirt. Ruby wanted to punch him in it, but Mama only raised an elegant eyebrow and said, "Just send me the bill." Like she was the Queen of England, flicking off a flea.

So he sent it. Ninety-eight seventy-five. They couldn't pay it, of course.

Two months later, when the mini oven exploded, he said they'd have to leave.

Their mother said it didn't matter. Who needed this old stinky place, anyhow? They should celebrate, that's what. So they packed all their stuff in the Purple Demon and drove to the Santa Monica Pier and rode the Big Wheel three times and the roller coaster twice and ate hot dogs and ice cream and walked barefoot on the beach and made up a song about a bean-eating grass-hopper:

> *Beans, beans, that's all I eat;*
> *I never get no jelly*
> *I hop and hop and eat my beans;*
> *So why do they call me Smelly?*

Pete just about fell down laughing at that, and Ruby thought it was pretty funny too. But her teeth were chattering a little; the red ball of sun had plopped into Mama's Pacific an hour ago. So they climbed back in the Demon and drove past a hundred NO VACANCY signs, until finally they came to a place called the Neptune Inn that had starfish bedspreads and pelican lampshades and mermaids on the shower curtain, and Mama thought it was so wonderful she decided they would stay there for ever. She called her cousin Sheila in Houston and laughed and laughed and said, "Oh, Sheila, you've got to come out here, we're living in Atlantis."

But Sheila couldn't come, and the mermaids turned out to be mouldy, and the next morning, Mama got sick.

Not sick like with a fever or the flu; Ruby would have known how to take care of her then. The kind of sick where you cry and cry and can't stop crying.

"Please, Mama," Ruby begged, "don't you want some breakfast? Look what we got you."

It was just a Coke and a packet of peanut-butter biscuits from the vending machines outside. Ruby had found eight wrinkled dollar bills and some change in her mother's purse. But for some reason that only made her cry harder.

"Look what we got you, Mama!" said Pete, his fist leaking crumbs. In his eagerness to help he had crushed half the biscuits to pieces.

"Thank you, baby," Mama tried to say, but it was no use. She gave a strangled sob and covered her eyes, as if the children's worried faces were small suns, blinding her. "I'm sorry," she moaned, pulling Pete and Ruby close, while great racking sobs shook her shoulders. "Oh, baby. My poor babies. I'm so sorry . . ."

For two whole days and two whole nights, she cried and cried and cried. She'd sleep a little, and then she'd wake up and cry some more. No, thank you, not today, Ruby told the maid. We don't need anything, not anything at all. And she wondered if this was what it was like when people went crazy, and what was she supposed to do if it was; and if you could die laughing like that old guy in *Mary Poppins*, was it possible to die crying, too?

And then on the morning of the third day, it was over. Ruby woke up feeling groggy and sticky (she hadn't gotten around to taking a bath without anybody reminding her), and with her tongue a bit tender from all those biscuits, and for a second she couldn't quite remember where she was . . .

And there was Mama, fresh from the still-steaming shower, up and dressed and with her lipstick already on, dabbing cream-coloured concealer on the circles under her eyes.

"Mama?"

She turned around.

"Can we go home now?"

Mama didn't answer right away. She opened the curtains and looked out of the window. Ruby came and stood beside her. The fog had rolled in. You could hardly see the ocean at all.

"Just wait," her mother said. "The sun's starting to work. I bet you we'll have blue skies by ten."

But the fog was thick, and Mama was wrong.

It took the sun till noon.

7

FADE IN:

The top of Mount Everest. A howling snowstorm in progress. ~~Five fearless Five stouthearted~~ A band of bold adventurers ~~struggles onwards and upwards through the thickly falling snow the whirling flakes the whirling, blinding bliz~~ stumbles blindly through the blizzard, following fearless OOLOO, their trusty Sherpa.

"Ruby! Have you seen the cap to the toothpaste?"

their trusty Sherpa guide. They are hardy. (But not foolhardy.) Exhausted, yet oddly ~~exciler exilarated~~ exhilerated. Also cautious. Yet confident. Cautiously confident. And extremely cold.

"For heaven's sake, Pete. I keep *telling* you to put it back . . ."

~~With every inch With every bloody step~~ Inch by bloody inch they climb, ~~pushing themselves past the limits, or what were till now the pushing past what used to be the previous the heretofore limits of human endur~~

"Ruby, have you seen the – oh, never mind, it was in the bin."

pushing themselves further than they would have believed possible before this day.

Ruby stops typing for a second and reads that over. Not bad. Not bad at all. Especially the part about the bloody inches. Sometimes she gives herself actual goose bumps.

Although it's kind of making her neck ache too. Pounding out this stuff on your mum's old Smith Corona is a lot harder than just dreaming it up in your head. But man, when she gets it right –

Inch by bloody inch they climb,

Well, come on. Is that chilling, or what?
Except . . .
Would you really *see* the blood under all those parkas and everything? Not to mention the rubber boots. Shoot. Ruby takes off her glasses, blows on the smudged lenses, wipes away the fog with the tail of her pyjama top. Maybe she should start with something even more

dramatic than climbing. Something like — well . . . maybe . . .

FADE IN:

The top of Mount Everest. A blinding blizzard in progress.

Suddenly — out of nowhere — a bloodcurdling

SCREEEEEEEEEEEEEEEEEEEEEAAAAAAM . . .

Mama puts her head in at the bedroom door. Her nose, anyway; she's all but buried under a basket of laundry. "Listen for the phone, will you, honey? I'll be back by eleven. And get dressed, for goodness' sake; if we're going to make the bargain matinee, we have to leave by eleven-thirty."

Ruby nods, only half-hearing. Saturday is always cinema day, if they're not flat broke after Mama pays the bills. The best day of the week. Ruby wouldn't miss it for anything. But there's still tons of time; it only takes her two minutes to get dressed. And she can't stop *now* . . . Where was she, anyway? Oh, yes, the bloodcurdling

SCREEEEEEEEEEEEEEEEEEEEEEAAAAAAM . . .

~~Five bold~~ Four horrified adventurers stand at the edge of a gaping chasm, peering down its icy walls at

~~the hideously smashed sadly pulverised bones of~~ the grisly remains of OOLOO, their ~~trusty~~ previously trusty Sherpa guide. ~~A good man, dead now. A good man, but dead~~. A good man, yes, but dead. Alas.

CUT TO OOLOO: Mouldering, yet frozen.

A knocking sound interrupts her train of thought. Is that Pete hammering ice cubes again? Ruby *told* him that's not how you make an igloo. No, wait – it's somebody at the door. "Get that, will you, Pete?"

Now CUT TO the new leader, LEONORA LYONS, ~~a girl but not a mere girl she of the raven hair and flashing black violet ebony~~

More knocking. Good grief. And Ruby's still sitting here in her pyjamas. "Pete! Would you please get the – oh, for crying out loud." Where the heck is Pete, anyway? He must have gone with Mama. Ruby gets up, pulls on a bathrobe, runs to the door. But of course by the time she gets to it, there's nobody there. Only a Salvation Army truck just pulling away from the kerb and some kind of flyer stuck to the doorknob.

Ruby pulls it off. "Thank you for your donation," it says. What donation? Ruby wonders. Mama didn't mention anything about putting stuff out for them to pick up today, did she?

Well, whatever. Maybe they leave these receipts even when you *don't* give them anything, just to make you feel guilty. Ruby sticks the paper in her pocket and gets back to work.

LEONORA LYONS, a raven-haired beauty with flashing violet eyes, which sometimes appear to be ebony, ~~depending on the light on her mood when she's really mad~~ when her ire is roused.

Except . . . hold on a minute. This is Mount Everest, remember? So Leonora's got on a hat, right? And goggles and ear muffs and a nose protector and who knows what all? So how are you supposed to see her hair and eyes, for heaven's sake?

Ruby chews on her thumbnail. Okay . . . how about . . . possibly no one *knows* she's a girl until they make it back to base camp and she takes off her headgear and her glorious jet-black tresses come tumbling down?

> FIRST CLIMBER (HAROLD)
> Good grief! It's a girl!

> SECOND CLIMBER (SHARKY)
> Well, I'll be a monkey's uncle!

> THIRD CLIMBER (LEROY)
> (humorously)
> Aw, shut up, Sharky. She don't want to hear about your relatives.
> (He gives LEONORA a wink.)

Hey, there, beautiful. What's a nice girl like you
doing on a mountain like this?

LEONORA

Special Agent Lyons to you, bub. Her Majesty's
Secret Service. We have reason to believe that
Double-O Seven has been kidnapped by a ~~lousy~~
~~rotten dirty stinking~~ rogue agent masquerading
as a mountain climber.

(a withering smile)

And you?

The front door opens and closes. "We're home,
honey! Are you about ready?"

Ruby jumps up and starts pulling on her jeans.
"Almost!"

Mama looks in on her. "Oh, Ruby. You're not dressed
yet?"

"It only takes me a minute, Mum. We've got plenty
of — oh, sure, Pete, just come on in, don't bother
knocking or anything."

"Have you seen Mammook?"

Ruby sighs and starts buttoning her shirt. Not that
she really has all that much to hide under there. "No, I
haven't seen Mammook." It would be nice to have a *little*
privacy every now and then, like a normal person.

But Pete doesn't take the hint. He just stands there,
looking worried.

"Where'd you see him last, baby?" Mama asks.

"In his time machine."

"His time machine?"

"You know, the one you said I could have."

"Oh. You mean that old box you had out on the porch?"

"It was his time machine. He was going to the Ice Age, so he'd be cooler. He's a *woolly* mammoth."

"Right. And then we went to the launderette. Did you take him with us there?"

"He didn't want to go. He thought he might get tumble-dried again."

"Oh. Well, then he's still in the box, right? Did you look on the porch?"

"It's gone."

"Oh, no, it's not gone, sweetie. You've just forgotten, that's all. You must have brought it inside, or – Ruby, help us think. Are you sure you didn't see that old box somewhere?"

They both turn and look at her, waiting for an answer.

"Ruby? Honey? What's wrong?"

CUT TO RUBY: *Mouldering, yet frozen.*

8

"Don't worry, baby," Mama keeps saying, as the Purple Demon wheezes its way down Van Nuys Boulevard. "We'll find him. I'm sure we'll find him. I'll bet you anything he's there."

Pete doesn't say a word. He's hardly said a word for the past forty-five minutes. He just stares out of the car window, his whole body radiating misery, like heat from a small, freckled fan heater.

There are *twenty-two* separate listings for the Salvation Army in the Valley phone book alone, including the thrift shops, the adult rehabilitation centres, and the service extension regional emergency aid. "This is an emergency," said Pete, perking up a little when they got to that one, but "I don't think they mean this kind of emergency, sweetheart," Mama had explained as gently as she could. And in the end, after all the wrong numbers and answering machines and well-meaning but mystified people who said she'd have to speak to their supervisor on Monday, Mama decided they'd better just head over to the nearest collection centre and see for themselves.

"Is that it?" Ruby asks, just before they hit Oxnard. It's supposed to be around here somewhere. But Mama says she's looking on the wrong side of the street; that's only some cemetery. This strikes Ruby as convenient. She figures if they don't have any luck with the Salvation Army, they can just drop her off here for burial on the way home.

Not that anyone has actually *said* the entire mess is her fault and if she hadn't been so caught up in her stupid screenplay and gone to the door when the guy knocked, Pete would still be your average, happy six-year old (well, happy anyway), and instead of being out on this desperate rescue mission they'd all be sitting in the cinema eating popcorn. But she's pretty sure she's not the only one who's *thinking* it.

Although Mama has to take some of the blame too. She said she told the man who called about donations last week that she did have a few old clothes and things she'd been meaning to go through, but she wasn't sure when she'd get to it. And he said that was okay, the truck was going to be in the neighbourhood anyway and they'd swing by, just in case. But then it had slipped her mind altogether after that . . .

"There is it!" Ruby yells, catching sight of the red and white Salvation Army logo on a building just ahead. Mama screeches on the brakes and makes a last-second left-hand turn, then follows the arrows around the corner to the Certified Collection Centre. Right beside it a big sign announces:

DONATIONS — THIS GATE

"There's the truck!" Ruby shouts now, her heart pounding with sudden hope.

"See, baby?" Mama smiles at Pete as they pull in the driveway. "Now, that wasn't so hard, was it?"

Oh, what a beautiful truck. It's just like Ruby remembers it, an enormous white whale of a truck, parked a little beyond the Homeless Service Centre on the other side of a tall chain-link fence. "That's it, all right," she says. "I'm sure that's it."

Only then — right behind it — she sees its twin. And then its triplet, just behind that. And then (her heart sinking again) its quadruplet, for crying out loud.

A moment of profound silence. Then —

"Well, it's bound to be *one* of them," says Mama, trying for brightness. "We just have to ask, that's all."

They climb out of the Demon and look around. The only person in sight is an old guy with a moustache and a potbelly, who's sitting outside the drop-off box, reading a newspaper. Mama takes Pete's semi-lifeless hand and starts over that way. "Maybe this nice man can help us."

How do you know he's nice? Ruby wonders. *He might be the biggest creep in all of greater Los Angeles.*

But Mama is right. The man is perfectly nice. He gets right up when he sees them coming and then stands there listening sympathetically while Mama pours out the whole sad story. "Yes, ma'am . . . I see . . . Mm-hmm . . . Well, isn't that too bad . . .? You say the boy has lost his — what did you call it?"

"Mammook," says Pete.

"His mammoth," says Mama.

"*Woolly* mammoth," says Pete.

Ruby feels the red rising. "It's a puppet," she explains. "From the Tar Pits."

"Got some tar on it, you say?" The man frowns.

"No, no, the Tar Pits. You know, the museum. Just off La Brea Avenue."

"Oh," says the man. "You mean the *La Brea* Tar Pits."

"You've been there?" says Mama.

"Can't say I have."

"Oh. Well . . ." Mama tries again. "Anyway, that's not important. What we're looking for is just a — well, a sort of hairy elephant-type thing, with curly white tusks and —"

"One tusk is broken off," says Ruby, "and Mama sewed on a button for the eye that fell out."

"Mmhmm. So in other words, it's pretty old?"

"Twenty thousand eight hundred and forty-two," Pete says quietly.

Mama touches his cheek. "We'll know it when we see it, right, baby?" She turns back to the man. "I doubt there'd be more than one in the truck, whichever truck it is. If we could just take a look —"

"Oh, no, ma'am, I'm afraid that's not allowed. Too dangerous, don't you see? We've got quite a bit of heavy equipment back there."

"Equipment?"

"Well, yes, ma'am, we have to unload the trucks into the carts — those are a pretty good size, let me tell you – and then we have to take the carts to the sorting room."

"I see. So we should go to the sorting room?"

"Oh, no, ma'am, you got to be a sorter to go in there. That's where they put everything in all your different piles, don't you see? One pile for furniture, and one pile for small appliances, and one pile for toys like that elephant-thingy you're after. And then you got all your clothes, of course. Your men's clothes, and your lady's clothes, and your children's clothes; there's always quite a few of those, as you might suspect. You know how fast these kids grow, both the boys and the girls. And then after everything's sorted out, it gets divided up again, don't you see, for all the various thrift shops. Why, from here it could end up in Culver City or Burbank or maybe even Beverly Hills – I know, I know, you wouldn't think the people who live *there* would be caught dead in a thrift shop, but you'd be surprised; plenty of those rich types know a bargain when they see one and we get some really nice items. Just last week we had a lady out here looking for her husband's brand-new Giorgio Armani dinner jacket. Poor thing, she was real upset; she said she'd intended to give us his old one. Of course I had to tell her I didn't like her chances of seeing *that* again. Oh my, yes, it happens every day, people coming over looking to find things they changed their minds about or their loved ones put out by mistake or whatever; it's the commonest problem there ever was, and we're quite used to dealing with it here, just as long as you go through the proper channels."

Mama is the first to recover. "There, you see, Pete, we just have to go through the proper channels." She turns back to the man. "And if we do that, then what would you say *our* chances are?"

"Of finding the elephant-thingy?"

"Yes, sir."

"Well, now, let me see . . ." He pulls on his moustache, calculating all the variables. "I would have to say, in this *particular* case . . . not too good."

Pete doesn't say a word. He just turns and starts walking back to the car.

"Pete, honey, wait," Mama begins. "That doesn't mean there's *no* chance —"

But the man shakes his head. "I wish I could say they were better, ma'am, but I have to be honest with you. 'And ye shall know the truth, and the truth shall make you free.' We don't want to hold out false hope to the little fellow, do we?"

"Sure we do," says Ruby. "He's just a *kid*." What is *wrong* with this guy, anyway? She glares at him and starts after her brother. "Pete? Pete, come back. He doesn't know what he's talking about . . ."

But he's already getting in the car. He's closing the door. He's locked it before she can get to him. "Pete? Please open the door."

He turns his back to her. He never wants anybody to see him crying.

Oh, man. Oh, Pete . . . Ruby looks at Mama and shakes her head.

"There's got to be *something* we can do," says Mama,

"someone else we could talk to who could give us permission or —"

"Excuse me, ma'am." The Moustache Man looks over her shoulder. "Just one minute, sir! Be with you just as soon as we get this lady's trouble sorted out."

Ruby turns around. There's a halfway bald-headed guy who's just pulled up behind the Demon and is unloading a whole bunch of stuff from the back of his Buick.

"Go right ahead," says the new guy, staggering a little under the weight of an enormous box. Ruby can see a jumble of satin-covered coat hangars poking out. "I'm in no hurry."

At the sound of his voice, Mama turns around too. And then her face changes. "Dr Dargan?"

9

The new guy goes red. Well, pink, anyway. Ruby has never seen a grown man actually blushing, but the poor doctor has turned this painful-looking shade of carnation pink from his neck to the very top of his not-quite-bald head.

"Mrs Miller? Well, my goodness, what brings you . . . I mean, what a very nice . . . How's this for a small world?"

"Good Lord. Mama *knows* this guy?

"And this must be your daughter?"

"Oh, yes, I'm sorry." Mama seems flustered too. "Ruby, say hello to Dr Ed Dargan. From the clinic."

Oh. One of the foot guys. Mama's been working there for nearly six months now, but Ruby has never met any of the actual chiropodists. She says hello automatically and sticks out her hand. (Mama drilled this into her skull before Ruby gave up on her dummy.) Unfortunately the doctor is having so much box trouble that he just about kills himself trying to shake it, first spilling a blue-flowered sundress on the pavement, then bending over backwards in a vain attempt to catch a teetering high-heeled sandal, before he finally gets the brilliant idea of just putting the whole thing down.

Man. Ruby thought doctors were supposed to be cool, like George Clooney. But then the Chiropody Centre isn't exactly a hospital. Mama *used* to work at a bookshop. It didn't pay much, but she got great deals on books, and at least their phone number didn't make Ruby cringe. Of course she knows she's being silly; a job is a job. But dialling 1-800-BUNIONS is almost more than she can bear.

Anyway, Dr Ed has solved his box dilemma and is shaking her hand now and saying, "Well, hello, hello, very nice to meet you. Isn't this something? I guess I'm not the only one cleaning out cupboards today."

Mama sighs. "I wish that's what we were doing." She looks towards the Demon. It must be hot in there with the windows up, but Pete hasn't moved. She lowers her voice, even though there's no way he can hear her. "I'm afraid we're having a little bit of a family crisis."

"Oh dear." The doctor's eyes follow hers. "Is there anything I can do?"

"Oh, no. No, thank you, Doctor. It's just a – a toy we've lost . . ."

"An elephant-thingy," says the Moustache Man, causing Ruby to jump a little. (She didn't know he was standing right behind her.)

And then they go through the whole thing again, and

he explains to the doctor why he can't let them go to look in the trucks because it's practically a life-or-death situation back there on the unloading dock, not to mention the sorting room –

"And anyhow, if the driver just picked up the thingy this morning, it wouldn't even be here yet."

"It wouldn't?" Mama and Ruby say together.

"Oh, no, ma'am. The trucks that went out today won't be back until closing time."

Well, shoot, thinks Ruby. *Why didn't he say that half an hour ago?*

"So, in that case, we should just – just *what*?" Mama glances towards Pete again. "Isn't there *anything* we can do now?"

"Don't the trucks have radios or mobile phones or something?" asks the doctor.

"Oh, yes, sir, absolutely state of the art."

"Well, couldn't you just *call* them, then?" Mama's voice is getting a bit strained.

"Why, yes, ma'am, we certainly could. Not me personally, of course. I'm not the dispatcher. But if you'll just go right around the corner to our Administrative Office, I'm sure they'll be more than happy to – oh, no, what am I thinking? They'll be gone by now, don't you see? It's Saturday."

"And on Sunday?"

"Closed on Sundays. We have church."

Mama takes a deep breath, then lets it out slowly. "I guess that doesn't leave us many options, does it?"

"If I can help in any way at all . . ." the doctor begins.

Mama shakes her head. She walks over to the Demon, knocks on the window. But Pete won't look at her either. So she fishes her keys out of her bag and opens the door. "Pete? Sweetheart?" She slides in beside him. Ruby stands back a little, giving them a minute. She can't really hear what Mama is saying, just the low hum of her voice, explaining and explaining. And then a long, terrible pause . . .

Finally Pete nods. Just the smallest of nods is all, the barest little bob of the head. Mama touches his hair (by now it's plastered down against his skull in short sweaty curls.) Then she steps out of the car again.

"I told him we'd have to try again on Monday."

"Is he okay?" asks Ruby.

"He's been better. But he'll be okay. He's Pete, right?" She gives the doctor her best attempt at a smile. "Well, it was nice seeing you, anyway. Sorry we kept you waiting."

"Oh, no, you didn't, not at all. I just wish there was something I could — well, listen, I'll bet you're all hungry. It's past one, and I'll be done here in no time. Does your little boy like Chinese food? Or pizza, maybe?"

"No, no, thank you, Doctor. It's awfully nice of you to offer, but we're fine, really. We've taken up too much of your time already."

"Not at all. It would be my pleasure."

Oh, for crying out loud. They're not going to have to sit in some stupid restaurant making small talk with an almost bald-headed foot doctor, are they?

"There's a burger bar just down the road," says the Moustache Man.

Good Lord. *No, Mama!* Ruby thinks at her. *The word is NO!*

"No, no, really, thanks so much, Ed. We'd love it another time. But I promised them a film this afternoon."

YES! Ruby can scarcely keep from shouting. That's what they need – a film! She thought they'd blown any chance of that; they missed the bargain matinee an hour ago. But one look at Pete's face makes it plain that doesn't matter today. What's a few extra dollars at a time like this? They've *got* to see a film, that's all. A comedy, if possible. It's practically an emergency, like he said before.

The doctor looks disappointed. "Well, I'm sure they'll enjoy that." He's gone even pinker than he was five minutes ago. "Another time then." He holds out his hand, first to Ruby – who gives it a quick shake and climbs in the back seat – and then to Mama. "So I guess I'll see you at the office?"

"Right," says Mama. "See you there."

Oh, for heaven's sake, come on, already. We can make the second feature if we hurry . . .

Mama gets in the car (*finally!*), waves goodbye, puts the key in the ignition. Ruby holds her breath while the engine makes its usual diabolical death rattle. You just never know with the Demon; they were stranded in the school car park on three separate Wednesdays in May alone. But this time it catches on the third try, thank God.

Ruby looks at the small red head in front of her. *Don't worry, Pete. It'll be okay. We're out of here. We're going to the cinema.*

10

OVERHEAD SHOT:

You're high above the Valley now, higher than the hills, higher than the tallest palm tree on Moorpark. From up here you can see everything — all the teeny-tiny cars and people, scurrying around like ants.

There's a little purple Dodge down there, hiccuping through the Saturday traffic. It turns into the General Cinema car park. Looks like at least half the county has had the same idea, but the purple car is crafty. It honks at a space-stealing estate car, then slips neatly into a narrow slot right up front, after a pushy green Cherokee gives it up as a lost cause.

Now a red-headed girl jumps out of the purple car and runs ahead to get in the ticket queue. Her mother and brother follow, a bit more slowly. As the three of them disappear through the door marked ENTER, a long-haired usher comes out of the door marked EXIT, holding a tall, skinny kid and his pint-sized buddy by the backs of their grungy T-shirts.

MOVE IN CLOSER . . . closer . . .

"And if I ever catch either of you in here again, I'll call the cops. You got that?"

"Yes, *sir*! Thank you, *sir*!" Big Skinny salutes.

"Roger, Roger!" says Mouse.

Big Skinny pokes him. "Who's Roger?"

"I thought *he* was Roger."

"No, dummy. *You're* Roger."

"*I'm* not Roger!"

"So who's Roger?"

The usher unhooks a mobile phone from his belt. "Funny, real funny. They're gonna love you down at the police station."

"Aw, come on, man. We're just kiddin' around." Big Skinny slaps the usher's shoulder. "You're doing a great job, you know that? You can't help it if your films suck. Can I please have my cosmo blaster back now?"

"Your cosmo blaster?" The usher smiles. "You mean *this* cosmo blaster?" He takes a red plastic glow-in-the-dark squirt gun from his back pocket.

"That's the one." Big Skinny reaches for it, but the usher won't let go.

He holds it up in the sunlight. "Very impressive."

"Top of the line," says Big Skinny, with a modest shrug. " 'Course it costs a little more, but I figure, what the heck? You get what you pay for, right?"

Mouse nudges him. "You didn't pay for it."

"That's not the point, Mouse. The point is, quality

counts. I'm talking long-term investment. You got to think about the future, that's all I'm saying."

The usher nods. "I know what you mean."

"See there, Mouse? *He* knows what I mean."

"Oh, yeah. I think about the future all the time. In fact . . ." The usher looks around, making sure no one is listening. "Just between you and me?" He lowers his voice. "I can actually *see* the future."

Big Skinny laughs. "Get outta here, man. Like that dude in *The Dead Zone?*"

"You don't believe me? Just so happens I'm seeing it right now."

Mouse's eyes go wide. "What do you see?"

"This," says the usher. He drops the cosmo blaster on the pavement and grinds it to pieces under his big black shoe.

"Aw, man . . ."

"That was top of the line!"

"You fellas have a real nice day, now." The usher turns around and goes back inside.

"Aw, man . . ." Mouse picks up a shard of shattered handle, then drops it in disgust. "What'd he have to do that for?"

Big Skinny shakes his head. "Some people just got no respect." Through the window they can see the usher bragging to the popcorn girl. She doesn't appear to be all that interested. " 'Course it could be we caught him on a bad day. They never like it when you squirt the other patrons. That short-necked fella with the crew cut was pretty upset."

"Well, he shouldn't have laughed at all those lame jokes, then. Ain't he got any taste."

Big Skinny pats his shoulder. "Easy, Mouse, easy. What are you gonna do? The Duke is gone, man. They don't make 'em like they used to."

Mouse heaves a sigh. "Worst film I ever saw."

"Well, it's always the kiss of death when the horses start talking. But let's try to look on the bright side."

"What bright side?"

"Just think how we'd be feeling if we'd paid to get in. Whoa!" Big Skinny stops in his tracks. "Do you see what I see?"

"What? That old car?"

"It's the Demon, man! It's *her* car! We watched the guy hook it up to the tow truck, remember? Look there – you can still see the clamp marks. And look, they've got that same sticker on the back." He points to the bumper.

PROUD PARENTS OF A HAYES MIDDLE SCHOOL HONOUR STUDENT

"Oh, yeah, that's the Demon, all right. I'd know that colour anywhere."

Mouse is unimpressed. "Okay, so it's the Demon. So what?"

"So she's *in* there, man! In the film!"

"Who? Miller?"

"Of course, Miller. Who else?" Big Skinny is getting agitated. "Come on, Mouse. We gotta go right now, before she comes out. This is the perfect time."

Big Skinny runs to the corner, where he's stashed his skateboard in a clump of decorative hibiscus.

"Aw, man . . . wait up, will you?" Mouse grabs his board and follows. "It ain't the perfect time, Big. It's broad daylight."

"Exactly," says Big Skinny, heading out across the car park past Solley's Deli. "Nobody'll be expecting us now."

"Aw, man . . ."

Mouse shakes his head, but he keeps on following, whizzing along by the office building that the psychic moved into after the murder and under the 101 overpass and through that maze of fake dead ends by the river. You can't talk old Big out of anything once he makes up his mind. But you can't just let him go off half-cocked either. Sometimes he gets the screwiest things stuck in his head. No telling what grief he'd come to if Mouse didn't keep an eye on him.

"You got to face facts, Big," Mouse reminds him, crawling after Big Skinny through the broken place in the fence that blocks off the truck entrance down by the bridge. The sign directly above their heads says:

PROPERTY OF
LOS ANGELES COUNTY
DEPARTMENT OF PUBLIC WORKS
TRESPASSING — LOITERING
FORBIDDEN BY LAW
UP TO $500 FINE OR SIX MONTHS'
IMPRISONMENT OR BOTH
STATE LAW

"What facts are you referring to, Mouse?"

"That girl ain't ever gonna like you. She ain't your type."

"She's not a *type*." Big Skinny gets through the break, then reaches back and unhooks Mouse from a bit of jagged metal where his T-shirt has stuck. "She's Miller. You don't know her, that's all."

"And you do."

"Better than you."

"Yeah, right. Like you know all the girls."

"She's not like the other girls. She don't hang around the mall." Big Skinny slides down a short gravel bank, then wades through the weeds to a little ditch beneath the roadside wall where half a cardboard box is upended. He lifts the side flap gingerly, checking for spiders. "She's smarter than that crowd. She's going places."

"Right." Mouse waves a dandelion out of his face. "So she'll be president of the United States, and you'll be — what? Minding the kids?"

Big Skinny thinks this over. "I believe I could handle it." He reaches in the box, pulls out a slightly corroded can of red spray paint. "I'd just take 'em to a lot of ball games."

"Oh, for Pete's sake . . ."

"Don't knock it, Mouse. Child care is an underrated profession. This is the twenty-first century; you got to keep an open mind."

Mouse rolls his eyes. "Listen to me, Big. That girl does not like you. She is never going to like you. Okay, so she ain't a type. That's only half the problem. It ever occur to you that you might not be *her* type?"

"Maybe not now . . ." Big Skinny starts back through the weeds, shaking the paint can as he goes. "But I can wait."

"Wait for *what*?"

"I'm trying to take the long view here, Matthew. Past upper school, even." They're back at the fence now, walking along the top of the river wall. "You got to give women time, that's all. Remember that film with the Duke of Ireland?"

"*The Quiet Man?* Sure. What about it?"

"Remember the red-headed girl in that one?"

"Are you kiddin' me? Forget it, Big. Don't be trying to compare Miller to Maureen O'Hara."

"Naw, man, that's not what I'm saying. All I'm saying is — aw, shoot, who's been messing with this?" Big Skinny stops and crouches at another break in the fence, this one wrenched up from the river wall itself: a thirty-foot concrete drop to the shallow green water. "It was wider before, wasn't it, Mouse? Come on, you grab that side. We gotta pull it up a little more."

Mouse kneels down and obliges. "All you're saying is what?"

"About what?"

"Maureen O'Hara."

"Oh, right. The red-headed girl. She didn't like the Duke either, remember? She was made at him for — what? Practically the whole film. But it all worked out fine in the end."

"It ain't the same thing, Big. It ain't even the same country. Listen, I'm sorry, I don't want to be negative or anything, but –"

"Time, Mouse. These things take time. Even for the Duke. That's all I'm saying."

"Time, huh?"

"Absolutely. Hold my feet now, will you? I believe we've got it wide enough." Big Skinny gets on his belly. "If I give her time, she'll grow to appreciate me. You'll see." He starts inching down the wall, spray paint in hand. "Maybe not for my brains . . ." Mouse lets him down just a little. "Maybe not for my looks . . ." And a little bit more. "Maybe not even for my sense of humour . . . Okay, that's far enough, Mouse. Hold it right there."

"For *what* then?" asks Mouse, bracing himself against the fence and holding on to Big Skinny's feet as if both their lives depended on it. (Which, as a matter of fact, they do.) "If you take away all of them parts of you, what's left?"

Big Skinny sighs. The blood is rushing to his head now. It makes everything clearer somehow. "The real me," he whispers, lifting the can.

11

MEANWHILE, BACK AT THE CINEMA . . .

The door marked EXIT is opening again. This time the usher is holding it for Mama, her arm around a white-faced Pete. Ruby trails after them, hanging her head.

"Thank you so much," Mama says to the usher. "I'm really sorry about the mess."

"No problem," says the usher. He looks like he's *trying* to mean it, anyway. "You come again when your boy feels better."

Oh, well. Ruby steps over a piece of smashed red plastic and follows the others into the car park. It wasn't much of a film, anyway. There wasn't really any point in staying to see how it came out. What are the odds on old Thunder actually *losing* the big race?

She climbs into the back seat of the Demon and closes her eyes. At least the beginning was good. She's crazy about beginnings. That moment just *before* the film starts, that's always the best. When the lights go dim and you're sitting in the dark with your popcorn. And then the music creeps in, and the lion roars, or maybe the moon kid goes fishing, or that tall lady just stands there, shining her magic torch. And your heart is pounding harder and harder, because at that moment *anything* is possible . . .

And then the film *really* starts, and the horses talk and your brother throws up.

Not that Pete was being a critic, exactly. He'd just worried himself into a stomachache over poor old Mammook.

"I think I'd better put him to bed," Mama says when they get home. "Listen for the phone, will you, Ruby? Come on, baby. We'll read your mummy book again, how about that?"

Pete nods a little and follows her down the hall. Ordinarily he's nuts about mummies. But Ruby can tell his heart isn't really in it now; he's trying to be polite is all.

Oh, man. Oh, Pete . . .

Why couldn't they just back up a little and start this day all over again, like in *Groundhog Day*? Ruby wouldn't need a dozen chances, either. Just one would do . . .

She goes to her bedroom, picks up her screenplay.

FADE IN:

The top of Mount Everest.

She drops it like a smelly sock. It makes her sick now. How could she have ever thought it was any good at all?

She walks back into the living room, switches on the TV. Channel 4 is interviewing racing drivers; Channel 6 is cooking omelettes. That makes her sick too, so she switches it off. She goes into the kitchen, opens the fridge, stands there looking at the Cheddar cheese. Talk about revolting. She slams the door shut. Everything makes her sick. The greenish water in the vase with the wilted daisies . . . the Magic Eye calendar with the swirly-whirly dots . . . the brown banana in the fruit bowl . . . even the dishes in the sink are making her sick.

Well, she can wash those, anyway, for her sins. That's better than nothing, right? She gets out the washing-up liquid, goes to work.

The dried egg on the very first plate nearly does her in.

Maybe she's *really* sick. Maybe Pete has an actual bug, some kind of horrible flesh-eating bacteria, and now she's got it, too. Only Pete will get well, because he's Pete; he's tougher than he looks. But Ruby will get even *sicker*. And they'll have to rush her to casualty, and Daddy will hear about it, and he'll fly in from whatever secret mission he's on and go running to the desk saying, *Where is she? Where's my little girl?* And the doctors and nurses will shake their heads and say, *We're sorry, sir, you can't go in there, she's having the last rites*, but he won't listen. He'll sock the orderly who tries to block him with a drip, and then he'll fight his way to her bedside. He'll push past the startled clergyman and grab Ruby's hand just as she's slipping away, just as she's going down that long dark tunnel (there's always a tunnel, right?) towards that beautiful bright, bright light. And she'll hear his voice calling her: *Don't die, Ruby! Please don't die! Speak to me, baby!* And she'll turn around then; she'll go running back to him; she'll open her eyes and say —

Oh, my God. Ruby stops stock still. The coffee mug she's scrubbing slips out of her hand and clatters onto a cereal bowl in the sink below. For a moment she just stands there, staring out of the kitchen window.

And then she comes back to life.

Stupid, stupid, stupid . . .

In half a second she's outside, she's tearing across the street, she's about to yell, *What are you DOING, you stupid jerks?* but then she remembers if she yells Miss Pierce will hear her for sure and then she'll see too, and Ruby doesn't want *her* to see. She doesn't want *anybody* to see. She's got to get to them, that's all. She's got to stop them herself, or she'll have to crawl under a rock and never come out again. She's got to make them wipe those stupid red words off the wall. They were bad enough before, but now she'll *die* if anyone sees them:

DEMUNS RUNS BUT YOU CANOT HIDE
IF YOUR CAR BRAKES DOWN
ILL GIVE YOU A RIDE

AND YOU NEVER HALF TO WORRY
WHEN THE RENT IS DUE
BECAUSE ILL WIN THE LOTTERY
AND GIVE IT ALL TO YOU

12

Run, Ruby, run . . .

But she can't get to them from this side. They must have gone down by the bridge. So she races around that way – very nearly ploughing into a couple of buggy-pushing mothers who are plainly in no particular hurry – and then she sees it, right under the TRESPASSING FORBIDDEN sign: that break in the fence, just a few feet down the embankment.

Well, sure, she sees it; the whole world can see it. All they have to do is open their eyes and *look*. Ruby can feel the cars whizzing along behind her, lifting her hair with the hot breath of their exhaust. How can she go down there in front of God and everybody?

But with the way the river curves from here, she can still see Big Skinny, dangling on the wall, adding the finishing touches to his masterpiece. He's done with the words and is boxing them in with a delicately scalloped border.

Steel enters Ruby's soul. (She recognises it right away. It entered Lady Lydia's twice in *The Whispering*

Heart.) She kneels down and fiddles with her shoelace till the mothers pass and the traffic thins out a little. Then she takes a deep breath, grits her teeth, crawls through the gap, and hits the trail running.

"*Stop that!*" she hisses, once she's close enough to make herself heard without screaming. She's crouching in the weeds now, just behind the perpetrators.

Mouse looks up. "Did you hear that?"

"Hmm?" All that shows of Big Skinny is a large pair of battered trainers. "Hear what?"

"It's me, okay? I'm right behind you." Ruby shakes the nearest stem. It turns out to be a dandelion. Little bits of white fluff rain down all over her head. "I said *stop that*, you morons!"

"Miller?" says the voice from the wall. "Is that Miller up there?"

Mouse nods. " 'Fraid so."

"Aw, man. It was supposed to be a surprise." Even from six feet above him, Ruby can hear Big Skinny sigh. "Well, come on, Mouse, pull me up."

Mouse does.

"Hey, Miller." Big Skinny dusts himself off and gets to his feet, staggering just a little. No doubt he's still a bit dizzy from the paint fumes. He grins sheepishly into the bushes. "What brings *you* here?"

"What do you think? Your stupid *poem*, that's what!"

Big Skinny looks puzzled. "Don't you like it?"

"Are you out of your mind?" Another flurry of white fluff. "*No*, I don't like it! I don't like it one – ah, ah, *choo*!"

"Bless you," says Mouse.

"Thank you," says Ruby.

"I sorta hoped you'd like it," says Big Skinny.

"Well, I don't, okay? You've got to wipe it off."

"Aw, Miller, I can't do that."

"Why not? You put it there, didn't you?"

"Well, sure, but — see here?" He holds up the paint can.

Ruby reads the label aloud: "Insta-dry?"

"It's the only way to go. That cheap stuff isn't worth a cent."

"So spray over it, then! Do *something*! You can't just leave it there."

"Aw, come on, Miller. I can't spray over it."

"Sure you can! You're not out of paint, are you?"

"Well, no, not quite, but —" Big Skinny breaks off there. He looks at his shoes.

"But *what*? What's your problem?"

Mouse gives her a poisonous look. "It's supposed to be in your honour."

Good grief. Her *honour*? Ruby feels as if she's about to spontaneously combust, like those guys on the Discovery Channel. There's no way around it, that's all. She grabs the paint can, runs over to the hole in the fence, kneels down, sticks her arm through, and starts spraying.

"Come on, Miller." Big Skinny tries to pull her away. You'd think he'd be stronger than she is, but he seems almost afraid to touch her. His hand on her shoulder is no heavier than the dandelion fluff. "Come on, please don't do that. It's dangerous. You could fall."

"Yeah, right, Spider-Man, you're one to talk." She jerks her arm away from him, very nearly catapulting herself through the gap in the process.

"Whoa!" says Big Skinny, catching her by the wrist in the nick of time. But Ruby grabs hold of the fence. No way she's letting go; she'll *die* before she lets go.

"Come on, Miller."

Ruby blots out the *D* in DEMUNS.

"I'm not kidding."

She moves on to the *E.*

"Please, Miller . . ."

The *M* is gone. The *U* is next; it's nothing but a flat red blob.

"*Cops!*" yells Mouse. "Run, you guys!"

Ruby freezes. *He's kidding, isn't he? Please let him be kidding . . .*

She turns around. The service entrance gate is standing wide open, and a black and white police car is bombing down the access path.

Oh, dear God. He's not kidding. He's NOT KIDDING!

"It's okay, Miller." Big Skinny grabs her hand. "It's okay. There's another bridge we can get to. The car can't fit on that one."

"Come on!" Mouse hollers. He's already fifty feet ahead of them. "What's wrong with you guys? *Run!*"

Run, Ruby. Right. Running is a good idea . . .

But when she tries to move, nothing happens.

"Come on," says Big Skinny. "It'll be okay."

Ruby shakes her head. "I . . . can't . . . move . . ."

"Sure you can," he says, but she can't – she really can't

– her legs aren't working, and even when Big Skinny tries to pull her along he can't do it because now *her* T-shirt is caught on the bottom of the fence, and he tries to unhook her but suddenly he's all thumbs; he can't get it loose.

"Just *rip* the darn thing," says Ruby, but for some reason he can't or won't or –

"*Run!*" Mouse screams. He's halfway to the metal bridge now. "What are you *doing*?"

"Go on, Mouse, get outta here!" Big Skinny hollers back, but Mouse isn't listening. He turns around and runs back and tries to help. He pushes Big Skinny away and gives the stupid T-shirt a jerk, and it comes off the fence with a loud ripping sound just as the doors of the cop car open and a booming voice comes over the loudspeaker:

"HOLD IT RIGHT THERE."

13

GO TO JAIL. GO DIRECTLY TO JAIL. DO NOT PASS
GO. DO NOT COLLECT –

"Miller?"

Like she's really going to *answer* him.

Big Skinny tries again. "I'm sorry, Miller. I'm really
sorry."

Ruby turns her head as far away from him as she can
possibly turn it and stares through the smoky glass of
the police-car window at the people on the street. All
the normal, carefree, unarrested people. Look how happy
they are.

She's back on Van Nuys Boulevard again. Talk about
handy. Turns out you can live an entire lifetime without
ever leaving this one street. The answer to your every
need within easy driving distance: the cinema, the
Salvation Army, the police station . . .

"You don't have to worry," says Big Skinny. "They
know me up there. They won't give you a hard time once
they understand. Me and Mouse'll do all the talking.

You won't have to say a word. It'll be just like it never happened."

Oh, sure. Ruby wipes away a hot tear with the back of her hand. Easy for him to say. He probably thinks of jail as a second home. But she will *never* get over this, never ever, not as long as she lives.

"They won't keep you overnight or anything. They have to fill out a couple of papers, that's all. And then you call your mum, and she'll come to get you. It'll be over before you know it."

Call her *mum*?

Great. That'll be a nice surprise for her. She's probably still reading the mummy book to Pete. She's probably just now getting to the embalming chapter. She probably doesn't even realise that Ruby is *gone* yet, much less about to be incarcerated.

Speaking of embalming, there's that cemetery they passed this morning. And Ruby thought she was having a bad day *then*.

Oh, Mama. Oh, Pete . . .

At least they didn't put handcuffs on her. She'd have died on the spot if they'd done that. But they wouldn't *listen* to her either. Not really. Neither one of them – not the blonde lady cop *or* her pinheaded partner.

Look at them, sitting up there in the front seat, on the other side of the bulletproof Plexiglas. They're not even thinking about their prisoners any more. They're too busy arguing about which one of their televisions was a better deal: her twenty-seven-inch Trinitron or the big-screen Panasonic he got at the discount warehouse.

Why couldn't it have been that nice policeman who came when Miss Pierce called? He'd have understood, Ruby was sure of it. He'd have believed her. But not these two. They couldn't seem to get past the fact that when they first arrived on the scene, she was the one with the actual paint can in her hand.

Well, that, plus she happened to be spraying the actual wall.

Okay, so it didn't look too good. But there were *extenuating circumstances*, all right?

"Tell it to the judge," the policewoman said when they tried to explain. She actually said those words: TELL IT TO THE JUDGE. What does she do, sit around watching old cop show reruns on her day off? Ruby would never in a million years write a corny line like that for an officer in one of her films.

Daddy wouldn't have talked that way. He'd have listened, *really* listened. He'd never arrest anybody who didn't deserve it.

But the thought of Frankie Miller only makes Ruby's throat ache even more. What would he say if he saw her now? What *could* he say? His own daughter, being hauled away like a common criminal. Sure, he'd believe her. But he'd be so disappointed . . .

It's all right, sweetheart. I understand. You didn't really intend to trespass or deface public property. You made a little mistake, that's all; everybody makes mistakes. But I still love you. Of course I love you . . .

"Come on, Miller. Please don't cry. It'll be okay, you'll see."

"Shut up, Big," Mouse growls. "Let her cry if she wants to. We'da got away fine if it hadn't been for her."

"I'm not crying." Ruby spits it out through clenched teeth.

"Yeah, right," says Mouse.

Even without turning around, she can feel him sneering.

In spite of Big Skinny's promises, nobody at the station seems particularly pleased to see him again. But then nobody seems particularly *surprised* to see him either – least of all Detective Donner, the dark-skinned, weary-eyed mountain of a man assigned to their case.

"What happened to Detective Fazio?" Big Skinny asks, when he and Ruby and Mouse are escorted into Donner's cramped office.

"Retired," says Donner, leafing through the three sets of printouts on his desk. "Last I heard he was raising llamas in Montana."

"No way. Fazio retired? He didn't seem that old."

"Stomach ulcers," says Donner.

"Oh. Stress, huh?" Big Skinny shakes his head. "That's too bad; he was a real good guy. Tell him I said hello, okay?"

Donner's upper lip twitches. "I'm sure he'll be thrilled."

Ruby makes a mental memo: *Burned-out detective with sense of irony encounters big dumb teenage –*

Oh, forget it. Although she probably really *ought* to be taking notes. There's great material here, if she just weren't feeling so awful. Where else would she ever get such an up-close and personal look at the inner workings of a modern-day police station? How else would she have ever guessed that the inkpad they use when they take your fingerprints smells like sour cherries, or how carefully you have to roll each finger from left to right so the lines won't smudge, or that the desk sergeant looks exactly like the Tin Man, minus the tin?

But somehow all of that is pretty cold comfort at the moment . . .

"You're *where?*" Mama said when she got Ruby's call. She and Pete (eyes big as dinner plates) must have broken every speed record in the Valley getting there. David Coulthard himself couldn't have made it in less than ten minutes.

But then he isn't Ruby's mother.

"It's okay, baby," she says, hugging her tight, when Ruby can't get her voice to work. "They've made some sort of idiotic mistake, that's all." She glares at Big Skinny and Mouse, then narrows her eyes at Detective Donner. "I don't know what lies these boys have been telling you, but there is no way my daughter —"

"Are you calling my son a liar?" This from Mouse's dad, a burly little man who has just arrived as well, fists clenched, temper blazing, smoke all but coming out of his ears.

Mama ignores him. "No way my daughter was consciously breaking any —"

"Mama . . ." Ruby tries to stop her. "You don't

understand. I was *sort* of breaking the – I mean, I couldn't help it. I *had* to . . ."

Mama looks confused. "Had to what?"

And then the words come pouring out, whole rivers of words, explaining and explaining, everything but the *main* words, that is, the actual trouble-making poem itself, which, thank God, Big Skinny is suddenly too shy to say out loud and there is not a chance in this world or any other *Ruby* is going to start reciting that mess, even if they *do* lock her up until she's old and wrinkled and her hair is all grey and matted and lice-ridden and her teeth are falling out, one by one by –

"Excuse me. They said I could find Vincent Bogart in here?"

Everyone – including Detective Donner, who has been listening politely through all of this, his expression never changing, and Mr Mossbach, who has been muttering under his breath the whole time, occasionally punctuating his opinions by boxing Mouse's left ear – turns towards the door, where the latest arrival is leaning in, looking worried.

"Ed!" shouts Big Skinny.

"Ed?" says Mama.

"Oh, my goodness," says the not quite bald-headed foot doctor.

14

FREEZE FRAME:

Detective's office. Chiropodist at the door.

And Ruby thought talking horses were hard to swallow.

"You know the *foot guy*?" she whispers to Big Skinny, so surprised that she momentarily forgets she's not speaking to him.

"Oh, sure." His face is shining. "Everybody knows Ed."

Well, almost everybody.

"Are you a relative of Vincent's?" Detective Donner asks the doctor.

"No, sir," says Ed. "Just a friend – with the Big Brothers Programme? The name's Edward Dargan." He glances at Ruby's mother, who smiles back, a bit uncertainly. No question about it, they're *both* blushing now.

Mouse looks at Big Skinny. "Didn't you call your grandma?"

Big Skinny shrugs. "She didn't answer. Prob'ly got her hearing aid turned off."

"I see," says Donner. He shakes Ed's hand. "Sorry, we're all out of chairs. But we're just about done here, anyway . . ."

Just about means another half-hour, as it turns out, while Ed gets brought up to speed on the crime and its consequences, which Donner explains in a voice so calm that he might just as well be discussing the importance of whale blubber in the life of the average Eskimo. But what he's actually saying is how dumb and dangerous and totally indefensible their actions were, and how Los Angeles County doesn't treat this sort of thing lightly, because not only is it a blight on the neighbourhood but also so often gang-related and possibly drug-related, besides which the river is a highly hazardous area that is strictly off-limits to everyone but the flood-control professionals, and don't they know that a teenager was killed just a month ago when he fell, trying to spray graffiti on one of the motorway bridges?

"It wasn't Miller's fault," Big Skinny points out. "She was trying to spray it *off*, not *on*."

But Donner stops him with a look and a brief definition of the word *indefensible*, which pretty much boils down to they can talk till they're blue in the face, but it won't change a thing. "The way I see it, you all have two options. You can either take your chances in court in a few weeks, in which case you might very well be forced to pay the full five-hundred-dollar fine *and* spend up to six months in one of our young offenders institutions – which I seriously doubt any of you would enjoy – or you can agree now to perform fifty hours of community service . . ."

"*Fifty?*" Mouse opens his mouth to object, then sees his dad looking daggers at him and closes it again.

"After which the facts of this case will be put in what we call a dead box for the next three years –"

Pete's eyes go to watermelon size. "A *dead* box?"

"An inactive file. And then removed from your records entirely, if – and only if – you commit no further offences during that time."

Good Lord. Their *records?*

Big Skinny raises his hand. "Is that three years from now, or three years from the end of the community service?"

Donner lifts a weary eyebrow. "Will it affect your plans?"

Big Skinny looks as if he's about to say, well, you never know, but fortunately Ed clears his throat and shakes his head in the nick of time, and for once in his life, Big Skinny takes the hint. "No, sir," he says, "I guess not."

They all accept Donner's deal, of course. What else are they going to do? Even if they didn't mind getting locked up for the next six months, nobody in this group has five hundred bucks to spare.

"Well," says Big Skinny as the others stumble out behind him, stunned and blinking, into the late afternoon sunshine. "That wasn't so bad, was it?"

He sounds positively cheerful. Ruby wonders briefly, if she murders him now, would it be considered justifiable homicide? How much would it add to her sentence? Wouldn't it be worth it?

Dr Ed is looking at Mama. "I don't suppose you'd care to – well, no, I guess it's still a little early for dinner . . ."

The guy must have a tapeworm. He's terminally hungry.

"I'm free," says Big Skinny. "We never ate lunch, right, Mouse?"

"Forget it, bub," Mr Mossbach growls, grabbing Mouse's left ear and marching him away.

The doctor scarcely seems to notice any of this. It's Mama's answer he's waiting for.

"Another time," she says with a glance at Pete. They both look as worn-out as Ruby feels. "But thanks, Ed. Really. I don't know what I would have done if – well, it was a comfort to see you in there, that's all."

Oh, come on. He didn't do anything but *stand* there. They'd have done fine without him.

But Ed looks as if Mama has given him a sack of gold, not just her hand to shake. "Small world," he says quietly, holding on longer than he has to.

You said that already, thinks Ruby.

"Small world," says Mama, smiling back.

Big Skinny turns to Ruby. He puts out his hand, too. "How 'bout it, Miller? No hard feelings?"

Trust me, says the toad. I'm really a prince . . .

"Forget it, bub," says Ruby.

15

FADE IN:

Main Street, Tombstone, Arizona. It's high noon, and the stagecoach from Dodge City is due. The nervous STATION MASTER is on the platform, pacing. He stops to check his pocket watch, then peers off towards the empty horizon.

ANGLE ON several large tumbleweeds, tumbling ominously.

Ruby skewers a soggy French fries carton with the tip of her rubbish-collecting wand and drops it in the large plastic rubbish sack slung over her left shoulder. As close as she can figure, she has gagged fifty-seven times in the last sixty minutes. No problem, she tells herself, taking off her glasses and wiping the sweat out of her eyes with the corner of the orange and white smock the county has so thoughtfully provided for her. Fifty-seven gags down, two thousand seven hundred and ninety-three to go. First she'll tidy up the entire San Fernando Valley, starting with this stinking park. *Then* she'll kill him.

ZOOM IN on a poster tacked up on the hitching post:

WANTED

DEAD OR ALIVE:

THE BOGART BOYS

ALIAS "BIG SKINNY"

AND HIS SHIFTY-EYED ACCOMPLICE,

"THE MOUSE"

FOR RECKLESS DISREGARD OF THE PUBLIC WELFARE

AND CRIMES TOO NUMEROUS TO ENUMERATE

YOU NAME IT, THEY'VE DONE IT.

$10,000 REWARD

"Hey, Miller, you want some gummy bears? Mouse found a whole packet over here!"

Ruby grits her teeth and holds her nose and stabs somebody's greasy old hamburger wrapper. Ignoring the Tittering Twosome takes considerable stamina. They've been goofing off ever since they got here, naturally, having idiot sword fights with their rubbish wands when they think nobody's looking. Between them, at most, they've picked up *maybe* half a toothpick in the last hour.

Of course, Theo, the sour-faced supervisor, keeps threatening to double their duty. She's got the other six delinquents in her charge — including Ruby — pretty well cowed. But nothing fazes Big Skinny and Mouse. You really have to hand it to them. Even on this team of losers, they're at the bottom of their class.

CUT TO the infamous Salty Dog Saloon. From behind its swinging doors come the raucous sounds of the outlaws' savage celebration: exploding gunfire and ear-splitting shrieks and hideously demented laughter. The plinkety-plink of an out-of-tune piano. Horses whinny in dismay. Thunder rumbles, though the sky is blue. Not a Godfearing soul is astir on the dusty pavement . . .

"Did you hear me, Miller? A whole packet! They weren't even open!"

Not a soul, that is, but Tombstone's one and only lawyer, the beauteous SUSANNAH WINFIELD. Head held high, she walks past the Salty Dog, oblivious to every taunt –

"Aw, come on, Miller, have one. I saved you all the red ones."

– taking no notice of the loathsome insults hurled her way.

"Unless you'd prefer lemon. Mouse hogged all the greens, but these yellows are pretty good."

A whiskey bottle shatters at her dainty feet. Bullets
whiz past her bittersweet curls . . .

"Miller? Aren't you hungry?"
"Forget her, Big. She ain't interested. Come on,
where's your dignity, man?"

Still SUSANNAH trudges forth, marching
purposefully towards the depot, where the Station
Master (CYRUS ABERNATHY) is shaking in his
boots.

SUSANNAH
No sign of the new marshal, Mr Abernathy?

ABERNATHY
N-Not yet, Miss Susannah. B-But you oughtn't
to be out walkin' at a time like this! Ain't no
tellin' what mischief them d-d-d-desperadoes
might be up to next.

SUSANNAH
That's why I'm here, Mr Abernathy. To show
the world that some of us aren't afraid to stand
up to –

ABERNATHY
D-Don't say it, Miss! It might get 'em riled!
D-Don't even d-dare breathe their names!

He tries to cover the wanted poster, his eyes
darting to and fro like terrified marbles.

SUSANNAH
Courage, my good man.

Firmly, yet gently, she removes his trembling hands
from the criminals' grotesquely grinning visages.

SUSANNAH
Look at those ugly mugs, Mr Abernathy!
   (He does. They shudder as one.)
Just a couple of two-bit crooks, that's all.
Once the marshal gets here, they'll be singing a
different –

"Uh-oh."

Ruby heaves a sigh. She hates it when people say uh-
oh. What's the big news now, a barely chewed tortilla
wrap?

But Mouse is chortling and pointing towards the ball
park. "Better hold on to your cookies, Big. The Girl
Scouts are here."

"Huh?"

"Ain't that No-Curse Burton over there?"

"Who?"

"You know, the Queen of Clean. That other stuck-up
girl from school. Old what's-her-name, Charlotte. Ain't
that her?"

Good grief. Charlotte Burton. She hasn't *seen* them,

has she? Ruby groans. Of all the rotten luck. It's bad enough being falsely arrested and convicted and stuck on this – this *chain* gang, but if Charlotte Burton sees her and spreads the word . . . Oh, boy, if *anybody* from school hears about this, why, she'll just never be able to go back there, that's all; she'll have to move to Alaska and change her name and start saving up for plastic surgery and –

Hold on.

Ruby shades her eyes with her free hand. Over there . . . that man on the other side of the park. The one looking all around, like he's searching for somebody. Ruby squints behind her glasses. She's seeing things, right? It isn't – it couldn't be . . .

Daddy?

For a second – or a minute – no telling how long, she can't move. Forget moving; she can hardly breathe. It *is* him. She's sure of it. Suddenly she's dead sure. Never mind that he isn't wearing his uniform; never mind that she hasn't seen him in five years. How could she have ever worried that she might not recognise him? There's no mistaking Frankie Miller. Not just his blue eyes – even from halfway across the park she can tell they're blue – or his size or his dark hair or any of that. Even if he'd gone bald she'd have known him anywhere. Something about the way he's standing there – just *standing*, for crying out loud. Something about the way his head sits on his shoulders. And his smile, that's the real tip-off. Nobody else in the whole world smiles like that . . .

"Daddy!" She gets it out finally, waving her hand above her head. "Daddy, it's me! It's Ruby! I'm over here!"

But he doesn't see her. How can he *not* see her? He's come here to find her, right? After all this time . . . Oh, she *knew* it; she *knew* he'd come . . . "Daddy! Here I am!"

"Is there a problem?"

Ruby turns around. Theo the Supervisor is standing right behind her.

"It's my dad. He's looking for me. I have to go."

Theo frowns. "You can't leave yet. We have two more hours. Tell him to come back at noon."

"I can't. I'm sorry, I just – I'll make it up later, okay?" Ruby throws down her wand and starts running after her father, pulling off the orange and white smock as she goes. "Daddy! Over here!"

But he *still* doesn't see her. He's turned back towards the ball park now, where Charlotte Burton has just struck out a snub-nosed batter. The crowd cheers; he's the last person out of the inning. The teams start trading places. Ruby cuts across the field to save time.

"Ruby?" Charlotte stares at her. "I didn't know you played ball . . ."

"I don't," says Ruby, running past. She can't stop now. "Daddy!" she hollers again. Half the fathers on the benches are staring now too, but Frankie Miller is looking in the absolute wrong direction. He's got headphones on, that's the trouble; he's got his music turned up too loud. Or maybe – maybe it's not just music. Maybe he's checking in with headquarters.

Maybe he's working undercover or something — well, sure, that's why he's out of uniform; probably he's on duty even now. He waves at someone in the distance, anyhow, looks at his watch, then turns away from the game altogether and starts sprinting down the jogging track towards the car park.

"Oh, please," Ruby gasps, "don't leave! I'm right behind you; I'm right *here* . . ."

But he's too fast for her. He's getting away —

"Which one is he?" asks Big Skinny, coming out of nowhere. "The man in the red T-shirt?"

Ruby nods and points. She can't catch her breath. "It's too late. He didn't see me. He's too far ahead."

"Don't worry. I'll get him." And Big Skinny is off like a streak. Or a stork — that's more like it — a great long-legged stork who thinks he's a roadrunner, tearing down the path, kicking up a cloud of dust, just like in the cartoons. "Hey, mister!" he hollers, threading his way through assorted weekend warriors, very nearly upending some guy with a beard and a big black dog and a silver-haired couple in matching turquoise track suits. "Wait up! Your daughter's back here!"

But apparently Daddy doesn't hear *him*, either. He just keeps moving relentlessly forward. He's practically at the car park now . . .

When Big Skinny makes a last desperate lunge and hits him with a diving tackle that sends them both sprawling.

Oh, God, he didn't hurt him, did he?

"What the —"

"Excuse me, sir. I was just trying to get your attention. Your daughter wanted to speak to you."

"My daughter? What are you, nuts? My daughter's at home."

"No, sir, she's right behind us." Big Skinny turns around and waves Ruby over. "I got him, Miller! It's okay, I got him!"

"Daddy?" Ruby pants, running to him through the dust cloud. "Daddy? Are you okay? It's me!"

But the eyes staring back at her are brown, not blue.

16

How could she have been so wrong?

"I'd have sworn it was him. You wouldn't have believed how much – well, at least from a distance . . ."

Pete sits quietly across from Ruby at the kitchen table, his peanut butter and jam sandwich untouched. He leans on his elbows, waiting for her to go on.

Ruby sighs. "It's no use. I can't explain it. You don't remember Daddy anyway."

"Yes, I do."

"No, you don't."

"I remember."

"Oh, come on, Pete. You were two years old when we moved here. Name one thing you remember about him."

Pete thinks that over.

"Just one thing."

He's still thinking.

"See?" A wave of bitterness rises in Ruby's throat. Or maybe there's just too much dill in her pickle. She can still see the startled stranger's face – half mad, half mystified — staring up at her from Big Skinny's hammerlock. Poor man was actually pretty nice about it, once he understood their mistake. Especially considering the nasty red scrape on his knee. At least he didn't threaten to press charges; that was Theo the Supervisor's helpful suggestion. And of course Charlotte Burton saw the entire scene too, so now the whole world will hear what happened. But Ruby doesn't give a flip about any of that. None of it matters any more. The guy wasn't Daddy; that's the only thing that hurts.

She shakes her head at Pete. "You were too little, that's all. You miss that dumb —" she breaks off there. She was about to say, *You miss that dumb puppet more than you miss your own father*; but she stops herself just in time. It isn't Pete's fault he doesn't remember Daddy, or that he's still grieving over Mammook. It's been two weeks now, and Mama has called the Salvation Army every day, but all the king's horses and all the king's men — and sorters and dispatchers and collection guys put together — haven't turned up a trace of the little woolly critter. Pete doesn't talk about it much any more, but Ruby knows he hasn't forgotten. He doesn't forget things — well, *some* things — so easily.

"I remember," he insists. Hard-headed as ever.

"Remember what?" asks Mama, coming in through the front door, balancing a huge stack of printed papers and envelopes on one hip. She's been over at Miss Pierce's again, helping her out with some club — the Friends of the Los Angeles River, it's called. Mama's never been a big organisation joiner, but Miss Pierce kept asking, and "Lord knows that poor old river could use a few friends," Ruby heard Mama telling Dr Ed on the phone last night. (Seems like he's always calling about something or other now. He's getting to be kind of a nuisance, if you ask Ruby. But of course Mama is too polite to say so, and he's her boss, besides. She can't very well tell him to take a hike.)

"Remember what, baby?" she asks again, lugging the stuff to the table and plopping it down next to the salt shaker.

Ruby gives Pete a warning look. There's no sense telling Mama what happened at the park, or trying to talk to her about anything to do with Daddy. She'd only get upset — that worried, close-mouthed kind of upset. She'd probably think it was *his* fault, somehow, just for looking like the other guy. And what good would it do? Think she's really going to start *explaining* things? Even Pete knows better than that. That's one door that never opens, no matter how hard they push against it.

Well, anyway, Pete gets the message. But he's also the world's worst liar. He just sits there without a clue how to answer, poking holes in his bread with his little finger.

"We were just talking," says Ruby, coming to the rescue, "about . . . you know, our old house and everything . . ." She points at the pile of papers, trying to change the subject. "What's all that?"

"Mailshots," says Mama. "For the membership drive. Ed and I can't go to the meeting next week; it's the night of Pete's birthday. So we promised to stuff our share of envelopes over here."

Wait a minute. Did Ruby miss a step? "When did Ed join the club?"

"Just this morning. He came by while you were out doing your community service."

Oh. Well. It's a free country, Ruby supposes. For *some* people anyway. Still . . . "Why can't *he* go to the meeting?"

"He's coming to the birthday dinner."

"*What?*" Ruby stares at her mother. "Ed's coming to Pete's birthday? Why?"

"I invited him, that's why. He's been so nice about everything, and, well, Pete said he didn't mind. I thought we'd make it a party."

Now Ruby stares at Pete, who takes a bite of sandwich to avoid her eyes and promptly chokes on it and has to be pounded between the shoulder blades. He didn't *mind*? Of course he minded! No way he wanted the foot guy at his birthday dinner. He just didn't have the nerve to say so, that's all.

Mama gives Pete's back a final pat, then starts fiddling with the club papers. "It's not . . . a problem, is it, Ruby? I just thought . . . well, you like Ed, right?"

Well, no, not particularly. Ruby doesn't say it out loud; it doesn't seem like very good manners. And anyway, she hasn't got much reason to like or dislike Ed, one way or the other. She shrugs. "I don't know. He's okay, I guess. It's just – well, we hardly know the guy, Mama.

I mean, sure, he's your boss and all, but that doesn't mean we have to – well, *you* know . . ."

"He's not just my boss, honey. He's a friend."

It's a perfectly normal sentence. There's nothing much to it, really. Nothing all that dramatic in the words or the way Mama says them. So why does Ruby suddenly get this weird feeling in the pit of her stomach? Mama doesn't . . . she couldn't . . . well, of *course* she couldn't . . .

"What about his wife? Is she coming too?"

Mama stops messing with her papers. She looks up in surprise. "Ed's not married."

"Sure he is! He wears a wedding ring, and – and that box he took to the Salvation Army – it was full of lady's stuff, remember? Satin-covered hangers and high-heeled sandals and – well, good grief, Mama, don't tell me those were *his*."

"He's a widower, honey. His wife died more than three years ago."

Oh.

So that means . . .

"You okay, Ruby?"

"Sure. I'm just . . . just not that hungry, I guess." She gets up from the table, carries her plate to the sink.

"You've hardly touched your sandwich –"

"I'll wrap it up. I'll take it with me. There's some stuff I need to . . . some research, you know, for my screenplay. I guess I'll walk on over to the library."

Mama puts a hand on her arm. "We're just friends, okay? You don't have to be concerned about Ed."

"I'm not concerned about Ed."

"I can uninvite him. If it's really going to bother you to have him here, I can make some excuse."

"No. Forget it. It's no big deal. I just . . . I just have all this research to do."

"Wait five minutes, honey. I was going to take Pete to get his new trainers. We can drop you off on the way."

"No, thanks. I feel like walking."

"You sure?" Mama's worry lines make her look older than she really is. "You didn't get too much sun at the park, did you?"

"I'm *fine*," says Ruby. She has to go outside, that's all. She has to get some air.

Mama holds on a moment longer. Then she nods. "Okay then. As long as you're sure . . ."

Ruby is halfway down the street when Pete comes running after her.

Man. Can't a person even take a stupid *walk* by herself?

"I thought you had to go and buy trainers."

Pete nods. He's a little out of breath.

"Well, go on back then. Mama's waiting."

"He could yo-yo."

"What?"

"Daddy. He could yo-yo." Pete hands Ruby a battered blue yo-yo, with the string still straggling from it. And then he smiles. "I told you I remembered."

17

Ruby doesn't go to the library after all. She starts over that way, fully *intending* to go, but the closer she gets to it, the less she can stand the thought of being cooped up inside those pink brick walls. She turns right instead, and winds her way back past Deano's Pizzeria and the Tattoo Emporium and the place where Mama does her grocery shopping, and then she crosses Ventura Boulevard and heads for the hills.

It's a whole other planet over here, south of the boulevard. The PRP – the Planet of Rich People, Ruby calls it. She's come this way so many times, she knows it all by heart. First you pass a jillion apartment complexes – LUXURY APARTMENTS, the signs say – with names Lady Lydia would love: "Chez Bel-Aire" and "The Carrington Crest" and on like that. And then you get to the regular houses – not too fancy at first, with a dog behind every fence (the funny little cocker spaniel that wags its entire body, and the poodle with the puff on his tail, and the worried-looking Dalmatian, who scares himself every time he barks).

And then about midway into the Domain of Dogs, you turn left at the sign that says "Mountain Laurel Lane", and there's a tiny blue cottage on the corner, where a fat, friendly black Lab comes racing out to the street, wanting to be petted, and an old man Ruby never fails to see is sitting on a deck-chair under matching palm trees, listening to some ballgame on his transistor radio.

"HELLO, SUNSHINE!" he roars, just like always. "HOW ARE YOU TODAY?" And Ruby smiles a secret smile, because they may *look* like a normal old man and his dog (Thelma, she's heard him call her), but they're actually the Gatekeeper and his trusty minion – the Guardians of the entire PRP – and they can't let Ruby continue on her journey unless she gives them the secret password.

"FINE, THANKS!" she hollers back, scratching Thelma behind the ears. And she keeps on walking . . .

And now the invisible gate swings open, and she's heading up her favourite street of all – the Enchanted Highway, she's christened it, though it's really not a highway, but a little twisting lane, like the sign says – where the lawns are clipped and the roses grow in perfect rows, and the sprinkler systems are turned on by invisible hands. There are even more dogs here – rich dogs, but they don't know it. They rush out all blustery and barking, just like their middle-class cousins, then stop short behind their wrought-iron fences when they see it's Ruby, and put up their noses to be petted too.

And then – all at once – the road starts to climb, and Ruby climbs with it, higher and higher, as it winds past ivy-covered wishing-wells, and garden walls dripping with bougainvillea, and the secret rushing sound of hidden fountains. Up and up and up, until Ruby is panting, and little lines of sweat are trickling past her ears and down her neck. Up and up and up, past the stately brown house with the glowing stained-glass windows and the grand grey house with the fat yellow cat on its roof and the beautiful pink house with the naked plaster lady on its porch (Ruby said hello to it twice before she got used to its being a statue).

And finally she's there – at the top of the hill. The top of the entire planet, as far as Ruby is concerned. Surely the grandest, most glorious mansion of all used to stand here, once upon a time. But it must have tumbled down the hill in the last big earthquake, because aside from a few broken bits of concrete, there's nothing left now. Nothing but tall grass and sticker bushes, and crows calling to each other from the telephone wires, and sky, and sky, and sky. And miles below her, stretching all the way to the far-off purple mountains, the whole San Fernando Valley is shining in the afternoon sun – houses and high rises and hospitals and all the rest of it – laid out neatly, like buildings in some giant child's model train set. Filled with perfect model people, leading perfect model lives, in a perfect world, where things never ever go wrong.

Ruby takes a deep breath. She calls this the Breathing Place. She can always breathe better up here, for some reason. And then she climbs down a couple of fractured steps to her secret sitting spot – a cracked-off piece of the old slab is all it is really – where the bushes with legions of tiny yellow flowers have grown up behind it on the street side, shielding her from the prying eyes of anybody who might pass this way.

She just sits there for a minute, breathing. Then she takes the blue yo-yo out of her jeans pocket and turns it over slowly in her hand.

How could she have forgotten?

It wasn't only your ordinary tricks that Daddy could do. He was better than that. Way better. Walk the Dog or Around the World? Nothing to a pro like him. Loop the Loop and Rock the Cradle? Baby stuff. Though of course Pete was too little to know the difference between easy and hard and just loved all of it. "More," he'd say after every trick. "Do it more, Daddy." And Daddy would grin and do another – maybe even the Texas Star, if he was feeling patriotic. That was a really fine one where he twisted the string around the fingers of both hands in double-quick time, and if you looked really fast, you could see the star appear, as if by magic.

Or maybe – if they were *really* lucky – he would show them Ruby's favourite: his special variation of the Man on the Flying Trapeze. That was the best and hardest trick of them all, so hard that even Daddy himself couldn't do it *every* time. He was going to teach Ruby that one. He promised her he would someday. But first she had to learn the basics, and it turned out those were a lot tougher than she'd ever dreamed. "That's the idea," he'd say when she *sort of* got the hang of it. "Don't give up now. Just keep practising. That's my girl . . ." Even though the truth was she really wasn't much good at all. It looked so free and easy when Daddy did it, just the simplest thing in the world. And when that little blue trapeze man spun through the air so gracefully, and landed on the string, and then bounced back up and twirled around *again* – why, Ruby and Pete had to cheer every time, that's all. You just never saw anything to beat it.

She stands up and stretches out the grimy old string. Then she winds it around and around, leaving a little give to it, just the way Daddy showed her. It's still got the old loop that used to go on his finger. Ruby slips it on her own finger now. Tightens it up a bit. Then she takes another deep breath . . .

But she's no better today than she was at seven. Better, shoot. She's gotten worse, if anything. A couple of sickly ups and downs, and that yo-yo is a dead duck. Or a fish out of water – that's what it looks like really, dangling on the end of the line. A poor little luckless blue fish, waiting to be fried.

There was a time when she thought Daddy must be dead. After the first few months in California, when he didn't come and didn't come, and Mama wouldn't say why. Ruby tried to call him, but when she dialled their old number, a recorded voice told her it was "no longer in service". So then she called the Wichita Falls Police Department, but Gladys – the dispatcher – said that Officer Miller didn't work there any more. And Ruby figured he must have gotten an assignment out of town or something, so she said, "Well, where does he work now? Can you give me his new number?"

That was when Gladys recognised her voice. "Ruby?" she said. "Is that you?" And Ruby said it was, and then there was a long pause, and finally Gladys came back on the line and said, "I'm sorry, honey. I don't have that number. I think maybe you'd better ask your mother about that."

But of course *that* was a big fat flop.

And then after a while Ruby got to thinking that maybe Daddy's new assignment might be secret information or something (by this time she was eight and could figure things out better). So she wrote him a whole bunch of letters and sent them to the police station with PLEASE FORWARD TO OFFICER FRANK MILLER printed on the envelope in big letters so you couldn't miss them. But she never got an answer.

And then one night she and Pete were watching this TV science show about organ transplants, and that got her wondering: What if somebody in your family died in an accident – say he crashed his car in a high-speed chase or got shot by bank robbers or something – and they took his eyes and gave them to some stranger, some blind person you never even heard of? And then one day you were walking down the street and you *met* this person, what would it feel like? Would he know you? Would you know him?

And that was when it hit her like a hardball smack in the head: that was what had happened to Daddy, wasn't it? Sure it was. That was why Gladys had that funny sound in her voice. That was why Mama was too sad to talk about him. He'd been killed in the line of duty somehow, and the doctors had tried to save him, but it was too late. So they took all the parts of him and gave them to people who would have died without them, people who would never have seen the light of another day otherwise. And now somewhere out there Daddy's heart was still beating. Somewhere his kidneys were filtering all the poisons from some sick man's blood. And somewhere his eyes were still opening every morning, looking out for blue skies and his girl, Ruby.

Well, it made sense to an eight-year-old anyway, even though she tried to keep it to herself. But when she woke up crying that night, and Mama heard and came in and held her, Ruby couldn't stand it any longer. "Daddy's dead, isn't he? I know he's dead," she sobbed. And Mama went stiff as a board and said, "Your daddy isn't dead, Ruby. Go back to sleep. It was just a dream."

But Ruby didn't believe her. She didn't know what to believe. Not until last year, anyway, when the phone calls started.

There had been three of them now, always in the middle of the night. She'd hear the ring and then

Mama's voice saying "Frankie?" And of course Ruby would be wide awake then, but Mama would never let her talk. "You'll see him tomorrow," she'd say. "He's meeting us for supper." And Ruby would be almost out of her mind waiting for tomorrow to come –

The first time, anyway. And the second, about six months later. And even this last time, just two weeks ago.

Still, at least now she knows for sure that he's alive. That's the main thing, right? The only thing that matters. Even if she does get sort of tired, sometimes, just waiting and waiting . . .

But one day it will all be different. One day *soon*. Ruby is going to see to it. She'll be the world's youngest and richest and most famous screenwriter, and then she'll be able to fix everything. She'll build a brand-new beautiful house for her family right here, on this very spot, on the highest hill in the whole PRP – only she'll build it good and strong, so there's no possible way it could ever fall down. And they'll have a dog of their own, and a flower garden for Mama, and a private puppet theatre for Pete. And there'll be so much extra money they can go to the cinema every day if they feel like it, and Mama can quit her job. And this is the best part: Daddy can quit his, too. He'll see Ruby's name in all the papers, and he'll realise he can retire from the CIA, and then he'll come home for good and tell the foot doctor to get lost, and he'll ask Mama to marry him all over again, and she'll say yes, and they'll live happily ever after.

Ruby takes another deep, deep breath. She gives up on the yo-yo for the time being. But she feels a lot better now that she's got her plan straight again. For a minute there, she had almost forgotten. She sits back down in her special sitting place and puts the yo-yo back in her pocket. And then she gets out the rest of her sandwich, and she eats every bite.

18

AERIAL SHOT: As the crow flies . . .

While the red-headed girl is polishing off her peanut butter and jam sandwich, the bird on the wire directly above her head gives one last disappointed cluck to its neighbour, then raises its wings and flaps away, hopping a handy little Santa Ana breeze and riding it down, down, down into the Valley, in a fraction of the time it took the girl to climb up. The crow had waited patiently, hoping she might drop at least a *crumb* or two of her sandwich, but no luck there. For such a skinny little squirt, she had quite an appetite.

Down and down and down glides the crow, all the way to more reliable territory – every San Fernando scavenger's idea of heaven – the kingly collection of bins in the alley behind the new mall.

He's just zeroing in on one with a partly open lid, where a particularly delicious-looking half of a hot dog is sticking out of its shiny tin-foil wrapper, when his trajectory is most rudely interrupted by a pair of teenaged boys (one long and gangly, one short and scowling, both unusually homely, even for humans), who are streaking through the alley on a pair of small wooden boards with wheels.

"Watch out, you dumb bird!" Mouse hollers, veering sideways to avoid the crow and very nearly careering straight into an illegally parked car.

"You okay, Mouse?" Big Skinny calls back over his shoulder.

"Yeah, sure," says Mouse, pulling up short. He checks his board for damage. Looks okay, although his wheels could maybe use a little grease; they're not turning as smoothly as they ought to. He gives them a kick to straighten them out, then takes another running start and zooms along after Big Skinny. "Dumb bird," he mutters again.

He's in kind of a foul mood, if you want to know the truth.

They're taking a short cut into the mall, where they're on their way to help old Ed with a shopping predicament. The three of them just finished playing a round of miniature golf over at Castle Park. Poor guy actually thinks people their age still enjoy that kind of stuff. Mouse doesn't care much for miniature anything; he gets teased about his size enough as it is. But "Come on, go with me," Big Skinny said to him after they were finally done with that community service nonsense. (They'd had to stay an extra half-hour, thanks to Miller and her bonehead chase.) "Ed won't mind." So Mouse tagged along, since he didn't have much else to do, except go home and stare at a baseball game on the TV set while his dad cursed the umpires and drank beer and told Mouse to quit sitting there like a lump and go wash the truck or something.

Ordinarily he'd just go hang out at Big Skinny's. It's better over there. Big's grandma never gives them any trouble. She's about a hundred and just takes naps, mostly, or watches the weather channel for hours at a time. Which is kind of a weird thing to do in Southern California, where "partly cloudy" is about as exciting as it gets, weather-wise. But Mouse isn't about to say anything. Big wouldn't stand for it, in the first place – he doesn't allow anybody to bad-mouth his granny – and she's a real nice old lady, besides. Plus she hardly ever remembers to turn on her hearing aid, so he and Mouse can do pretty much whatever they feel like.

Still, there wasn't any point going over there by himself, so when Big said come on, Mouse said okay. But if he'd known about this whole shopping part of the deal, not to mention kamikaze crows, he might have made that a no, thanks.

"You think a seven-year-old would like draughts?" Ed asks them when they finally catch up with him inside the mall. He's standing in front of an entire wall of board games in the biggest toy shop you ever saw, looking as out of it as, well, as an old guy in a toy shop. He's got to go to Ruby Miller's little brother's birthday party next Wednesday, and he doesn't have a clue about what kind of present he ought to take.

"How 'bout one of them T-shirts that say stuff?" says

Mouse. "You know, like, 'I'm with Her Majesty'?" It seems like a reasonable suggestion, considering who the poor kid's sister is.

But Big never does have much of a sense of humour when it comes to Miller.

"Come on, Mouse. This matters, okay?"

Mouse sighs. "Man, can't anybody take a joke any more?"

But he tries to help after that. He really does. He stands there staring at racing cars and train sets and magic kits and water rockets and all kinds of cool stuff he wouldn't half mind getting for himself (well, if he was seven) until he's practically cross-eyed. But old Ed's just so worried about choosing the wrong thing that he can't make up his mind.

"What about one of these?" Big Skinny asks when they get to a rack with a bunch of really gross-looking monster puppets hanging on it, and Ed seems interested at first, but then he says, well, no, maybe not, and tells them this long, long story about how the kid's lost this mouldy old puppet he was nuts about, and maybe they'd better not get him something too close to that because it might just make him sad. So anyhow, they're stuck in here for more than an hour, and the whole thing's nothing but a big waste of time, and Mouse can't even get the new cosmo blaster he's had his eye on because old Ed is sharper than he looks and takes one glance at the bulge under Mouse's T-shirt and makes him put it back. And finally Ed says he guesses maybe he'll just try again later; he has to go run a couple of other errands, and would they like to come along or can he drop them at home or somewhere, but they say, no, thanks, they have their boards. So then he says goodbye and Big Skinny and Mouse goof around in the mall a while longer. And while they're standing out in front of the Cheesecake Factory, pretending to be conducting a survey for the Health Department (asking stuffed-looking customers who are staggering out with their doggy bags if their dining experience was enjoyable, and is there any truth at all to the rat rumours, and have they seen any evidence whatsoever of termite eggs in the raspberry mousse surprise), Big Skinny looks at Mouse and says, "I know how to find out what Miller's brother wants for his birthday."

"How?" asks Mouse.

Big Skinny shrugs. "We'll ask him."

So here they are, like a couple of all-day suckers, off on another one of old Big's doomed missions. Trying to go through the kid brother to get on Miller's good side again. Not that Big was ever there to start with, as Mouse had *tried* to point out on numerous occasions. But you think he'd listen?

Look at the poor jerk. He's still limping a little from tackling that guy for her this morning. "She thought it was her dad," was the only thing he'd say about it. He didn't even mind getting busted up and yelled at, all on Miller's account. And for what? You think she's grateful? Fat chance. About as grateful as she was that day at the river when the cops came and she got stuck on the fence. Mouse knew there wasn't any sense staying there with her. Think *she'd* have stayed if it was the other way around? If Big and Mouse were the ones in trouble? Yeah, right. They're just a couple of morons, that's all she thinks. That's all she's ever gonna think. But old Big still wouldn't leave her, the big dope. He never will leave anybody. He wouldn't leave Mouse either, that time he fell through the hole in the roof of that condemned house they were checking out after the earthquake. Mouse told him to go, but he wouldn't. He went and called an ambulance, and then he came back and sat right there till it came, because he's nothing but a big dummy, that's all he is. So of course Mouse can't leave *him* now, even though he knows they're heading straight into enemy territory . . .

"She's not home," says a voice from nowhere, when they're halfway up Miller's porch steps.

"Huh?" Mouse and Big look around, but they can't see anybody.

"My sister," says the voice. "She's not here."

Big nudges Mouse and points towards their feet. Mouse sees him then – it's the kid himself, sitting under the stairs, drawing in the dirt with a little pointed stick.

"Hey," says Big, limping back down and squatting beside him. "Whatchya doin' under there?"

"Research," says the kid.

Research? Mouse looks at Big. This is definitely Miller's brother.

"You could go to the library," says the kid, his eyes still on his work. "That's where she went."

"That's okay," says Big. "We came to see you."

The kid stops drawing. He looks up now – not suspiciously exactly, but not exactly unsuspiciously either. "Me?"

"Sure," says Big. "You're Pete, right?"

The kid nods.

"Pete Miller? You'll be seven years old on Wednesday?"

He nods again.

Big points to himself. "You know who I am?"

"Yep," says Pete. "You got my sister arrested."

Big sighs. "Sorry about that."

"I saw you at the jail."

"Well, not the jail exactly. Technically, that was just the police station." Big puts out his hand. "I'm Vincent."

Pete hesitates a couple of seconds. Then he shakes it.

"And this here's Mouse – Matthew." Big looks at Mouse. Mouse rolls his eyes, then sticks out his hand too. Pete thinks its over. Shakes it. Goes back to his stick drawing.

Big leans over, trying to see it better. Looks like the kid is tracing his own feet. "So what kind of research is it?"

"Shoes," says Pete.

"Shoes?"

Pete points to a battered pair of trainers to his left. "Old shoes . . . new shoes." He taps the bright red pair he's wearing now. "Half an inch bigger. First I measure 'em, then I test 'em."

Big Skinny nods. "Half an inch, huh? How long did that take?"

"Six months." Pete shrugs like it's no big deal.

Dumb kid, thinks Mouse. But he feels a kind of pang. He used to test his shoes too, when he was young.

"Not bad," says Big. "You timed 'em yet?"

"Sure," says Pete.

"The new ones are faster, right?"

"Oh, yeah."

"By how much?"

"Two."

"Two seconds?"

"I think so. I counted to ten in the old ones, and only to eight in the new ones. From here to the end of the street."

"You just counted? Didn't you check it out on your watch?"

Pete sighs. "I tried. The hands don't go fast enough." He holds out his wrist to show them his watch: one of those old Disneyland models.

"Oh." Big looks at Mouse and shakes his head. "Hear that, Mouse? No second hand."

"Bummer," says Mouse. Are they going to spend the rest of the day here or what?

"You have a second hand on *your* watch, don't you Mouse?"

"Hmm? Oh. Yeah, I guess so."

"Well, come on, then, what are we waiting for? If you're gonna do research, you got to do it right."

Aw, man. How's any of this supposed to help old Ed figure out what to get the kid for his birthday? Personally, Mouse doesn't get the connection, but you never saw seven-year-old eyes light up so fast. So of course now they're stuck *here* for another half-hour, while Pete races back and forth down the street: first in his new shoes, then in his old shoes, then in his new shoes again. (Of course he always tries a little harder in those, so naturally they always turn out to be speedier. But Mouse doesn't bother to point this out. It's pretty much all you got going for you when you're only seven.) And meanwhile they're timing him with Mouse's watch, and writing the results in the ground next to the matching outlines, and old Pete is having such a good time that even Mouse can't help kind of rooting for him – you know, just a little bit – over on the side. And somewhere in there he looks behind him and notices that the kid's mother and the old lady with the bird have both come out on the porch and are watching the speed trials too. And Mouse gets kind of nervous then. (If he recalls correctly, down at the station, Mrs Miller didn't seem to care much for him, or for Big either. And the last time they saw old Prune Face, she was definitely ticked off.) But the ladies don't appear to be all that upset any more. They're even kind of smiling, until –

"What are you guys doing here?"

Mouse was looking the wrong way; he didn't see her coming. Now she's standing right beside him, glaring: the Snob Queen herself.

"Hey, Miller," shouts Big, waving, as he half trots, half limps back from the corner behind Pete, who has just broken the new-shoe record by a quarter of a second.

"I asked you what you're doing here?"

"Research," Pete pants. He's still out of breath from his victory lap.

"Come on, Big," says Mouse. "Fun's over."

Big just stands there for a second or two, looking at Miller like there's something else he wants to say. But the scowl on her face doesn't help him any, so finally he turns to Pete. "Okay then, champ. You keep working, you hear? Heel to toe, just like I showed you."

"Heel to toe," says the kid.

Big and Mouse grab their boards and start to head out. Then Big turns around. "I forgot to ask you," he says to Pete. "Anything special you want for your birthday?"

"A time machine," says Pete.

A *time machine*? Mouse looks at Big. Old Ed's gonna be thrilled with that one.

"Okay," says Big. "See you at the party."

"The *party*?" Ruby wails, as Big and Mouse zoom away.

19

FADE TO BLACK: And utter silence.

And yet, not totally utter.

Somewhere in the darkness, a storm is raging.
You can hear it if you listen closely: the pounding of
the pouring rain, the mournful moaning of the
wind. And through it all, the desperate drumbeat of
a lone human heart –

> Ba-bump . . . ba-bump . . .
> Ba-bump . . . ba-bump . . . ba –

BOOM!

THUNDER CRASHES, cleaving the night asunder.
Lightning RIPS across the sky in a jagged streak. By
the glow of its eerie incandescence, you can just
make out the image on the screen: a great, gloomy
castle, perched high atop some nameless cliff, above

the seething, churning waters of some equally
nameless ocean.

A velvet voice begins to speak. We'll call her M, for
now:

M

We were an odd assortment, that was obvious
from the outset. Drawn, one might say, from the
devil's own drawer of mismatched socks. Five
complete strangers, summoned to this remote
manor house on the fabled Coast of Caldamoora
by the invitation of its reclusive (and as rumour
had it, possibly deranged) master: Peter the
Unfathomable, that most mysterious of earls,
old "Its-My-Party-and-I'll-Ask-Whatever-Idiots-I-
Feel-Like" Pete himself . . .

"Ruby! Are you done with those balloons yet, honey?
Ed and the boys will be here any minute!"

Ruby sighs and lets a little air out of a large blue
Mickey Mouse head. She's overblown it a bit; it's so full
she can hardly manage the knot. "Just about," she calls
back, even though there are still about twenty balloons
left in the bag. In a burst of birthday enthusiasm, Mama
got carried away and bought the giant economy size.
Ruby has huffed and puffed so hard in the last half-hour,
she can hardly see straight.

Which is pretty darn sporting of her, if she does say
so herself, especially under the mind-boggling circum-

stances. She still cannot *believe* Pete would invite those guys to his party. What in the world could he possibly have been *thinking*?

M

"An invitation to a night of terror," our engraved cards had read. "The Great Masked Ball of Caldamoora: the ultimate Dance with Destiny. Solve the puzzle and win the prize: a million dollars and the deed to the manor. Fail, and you lose all. Yet answer me this riddle: If truth be told, what have you left to lose?"

The balloon slips through Ruby's fumbling fingers and goes flying away, hissing and hurtling around the living room like a crazed rocket. The place does look pretty great, she has to admit – all dolled up in crêpe-paper streamers and those little white lights they always put up at Christmas, just waiting for the balloons as the finishing touch. Mama took the whole afternoon off from the clinic to get everything ready, and Ruby helped, once she got home from her latest prison detail: three fun-filled hours of painting over graffiti on assorted community-owned walls. Though not, unfortunately, on the one wall she would gladly *kill* to paint over . . .

The balloon splutters to a landing on the kitchen window-sill. Ruby sighs and picks it up and starts blowing again, her eyes going to those dumb red words no matter how hard she tries not to look.

NS RUN BUT YOU CANOT HIDE

Even after nearly three weeks, they still make her want to crawl under a rock somewhere.

"Why *those* guys?" she had practically howled at Pete. "Why not some of the boys from your school?"

Not that Pete had a whole army of buddies to choose from. He was sort of on the shy side, to tell you the truth. Which worried Mama, just a little, from time to time. But still . . .

"What about Danny Rendich? Or Ross McMahon?"

Pete shrugged. "They both went to camp."

"Well, *anybody*, then. Anybody but Big Skinny . . ."

"He said he was sorry."

Ruby just stared at him. Sorry? What good is sorry? Except to the person saying it? Oh sure, it's a great deal for *that* guy. Just do whatever brainless thing you feel like doing, stomp all over whoever you feel like stomping, then just say "Sorry," and everything is fine and dandy, no sweat.

Ruby stretches out the blue balloon and starts blowing again.

M

"Regrets only," said the card. Ah, yes. The coward's way out. Yet the riddle cut close to the bone. "If truth be told –" each of us had some dark secret. Would this night be our salvation? Or our doom?

Ba-bump . . . ba-bump . . .
Ba-bump . . . ba-bump . . . ba –

"Ruby! Did you – oh, that's plenty, sweetheart. Those are beautiful; we can save the rest. Now, where did I put that string? It was right – oh, here it is. Okay, if you'll just hold this chair steady for me, I'll tie this whole bunch over the table . . . That's the way . . . Well, look at that, aren't they pretty? Doesn't everything look wonderful? Oh, thank you, honey. I hope you didn't make yourself dizzy. Would you like to lie down for a while? I passed right out blowing up balloons once when I was about your age . . ."

M

First on the scene was Lady Pearl Fairhaven, chattering brightly – perhaps a touch TOO brightly. Renowned both for her great beauty and her woefully empty purse, Lady Pearl was no stranger to dire straits, especially since the disappearance of her noble husband, Lord Fairhaven, world-famous archaeologist, last seen entering the fabled tomb of Khufu the Accursed, who (as fate would have it) was at this very moment –

A knock at the door sends Mama running back to her bedroom, grabbing curlers out of her hair as she goes. "Oh, my goodness, they're here! And I'm not half ready; I still have to ice the cake, and – Ruby, will you get that,

honey? Pete! Pete, did you wash your face, baby? Your
guests have arrived!"

Man. You'd think it was the president of Paramount.
Ruby takes a deep breath, steels herself for the dreaded
onslaught. Then she marches grimly to the door, gives
the handle a turn . . .

M
(her voice ashen)

Great Godfrey's ghost. Even I – Sherlock Miller
– who thought I had seen everything, was
appalled by the repugnant trio who now met
my horrified gaze:

(1) Eduardo the Boring: A man of stupefying
dullness.

(2) "Little" Matthew Sneak Thief: Mean as a
snake. Clearly on the lam.

(3) Vincent "The Poet" Skinerovsky: Escaped
only recently from the lunatic asylum.

Had they donned their masks already, or did
they always look like that?

"Hey, Miller! What's up?" Big Skinny's big dumb
face is wreathed in smiles. "Where's the birthday boy?"

"Here," says Pete. And here he is, appearing out of
nowhere all of a sudden, standing at Ruby's side in his

new red trainers. Looking pleased and shy at the same time –

Which as it happens is pretty much exactly how Ed looks. "Happy birthday, Pete," he says, handing him a small, neatly wrapped package (the bow is bigger than the box), "and many happy returns."

"Happy birthday," Mouse mutters.

"Way to go, champ," says Big Skinny, and they hand Pete their presents, too. (Ed didn't help them with their wrapping, that's for sure; it's definitely on the scabby side. Ruby notices a couple of fat Santa Clauses winking at her from under the squashed bow on Big Skinny's lumpy offering.)

"Thanks," says Pete, carrying all the gifts over to the table and adding them to the others already laid out there.

Ruby spots the daisies then, peeking out from behind Ed's back. Rats. Of all the rotten luck. Mama's nuts about daisies. "For our hostesses," he says, holding them out.

"Thanks," says Ruby. Then she hurries them over to the kitchen sink and sticks them in a jam jar in the corner, where they shouldn't attract *too* much attention, anyway.

"Ready to check out your loot?" Big Skinny asks Pete, eyeing the presents with considerable interest. If he weren't twelve feet tall, you'd think he was the year-three guy here.

But Ruby sets him straight. "Dinner first. Then he blows out his candles. *Then* presents."

"Hear that, Big?" Mouse wags a finger under Big Skinny's nose. "Food first, presents later. Those are the *rules*, Private!"

Which makes Ruby's cheeks burn for some reason. But Big Skinny thinks it's hilarious. "*Yes*, sir! Thank you, sir! I will stick to the programme, *sir*!"

Man. What a couple of jerks.

"Well, Pete," says Ed, trying to change the subject, "how does it feel to be seven?"

"Okay," says Pete.

Big Skinny picks up a tortilla chip and dips into the guacamole. "His feet are half an inch longer than they were six months ago," he says, nodding wisely. There's a large glob of green on the end of his nose. "And you ought to see him run the twenty-five-yard dash. You been practising, champ?"

Ruby narrows her eyes at him. If he's making fun of her brother, she'll have to strangle him, that's all, party or no party. But he doesn't *look* like he's teasing, and Pete – who can generally spot a phoney a mile away – doesn't seem insulted. He's nodding too, is what he's doing. "Heel to toe."

"Good man," says Big Skinny.

"Well, isn't this fun?" Mama sweeps in, beaming and shaking hands all round, in her best Miss Witchita Falls mode. "Welcome, welcome, so glad you could all come. Does everyone know everyone? Can I get you some iced tea or lemonade, or – Ruby, did you offer our guests something to drink?"

Oh, come on, Lady Pearl, you don't have to overdo it . . .

But old Eduardo lights up like a Christmas tree. And no wonder. Mama does look awfully nice, Ruby can't help noticing. Maybe a little *too* nice. Did she really have to wear the *green* dress? Wouldn't she have been more comfortable in something a little more – well, a little more like jeans and an old sweatshirt?

Ruby glances nervously at Ed, who appears to have lost all power of speech. He suddenly looks a little like a seven-year-old himself. A partly bald and extremely pink-faced seven-year-old. He's got hold of Mama's hand again; he's clamped on to it like a snapping turtle. *Will he hang on till it thunders?* Ruby wonders. *And is his own hand still clammy?* She hopes so, anyway. It was clammy when she shook it five minutes ago. That at least would be *some* comfort.

"Oh, my goodness, look at the daisies! Did you bring these? Oh, how nice, Ed; how did you know? Daisies are our favourites, aren't they, Ruby?"

And with that Mama leaves the poor guy nodding and smiling like one of those not-terribly-intelligent-looking bobble-head dolls and rushes over to the dumb daisies and whips them right out of that old jam jar and into her best blue vase and puts them right smack bang in the middle of the birthday table.

Shoot.

But there's nothing Ruby can do about it now, and this is Pete's night, after all, and as long as *he's* happy – well, she doesn't want to ruin it for him by being grouchy about every little thing. So she sets her jaw and tries to smile and does her best to be pleasant and help out with the serving, and they all make it through the next hour or so without any major catastrophes.

CUT TO the banqueting hall . . .

"You fried this chicken yourself, Mrs Miller?" Big Skinny reaches for his fourth drumstick. "Man, it's practically as good as KFC!"

"Thank you, Vincent," says Mama, smiling behind her camera and clicking snapshots – first of Pete, then the other kids, then Ed, who returns her smile while choking on a bite of biscuit.

"You okay, Ed?" asks Big Skinny, pounding him on the back.

"Fine," Ed wheezes, wiping the tears out of his eyes. He looks at his hostess and grins. "Better than fine."

Ruby manages not to groan.

"The potato salad's real good too," Big Skinny goes on, blissfully unaware that his conversation might be anything less than sparkling. "Look at old Pete puttin' it away. That's right, champ – that's your carbohydrates, you know that? Got to have plenty of those when you're in training." He grins and elbows Mouse. "Lucky thing there's no eyeballs in there, right, Mouse?"

"*Eyeballs?*" says Pete, his own pair widening considerably.

Mouse snickers softly into his coleslaw.

"You know," says Big Skinny, "one of them fake eyeballs you can get at the joke shop. You've been over there, right, champ?"

Pete shakes his head.

"Aw, man, you never been to Floddenfield's? You gotta see this place. They got everything – all the classics – fake vomit, and fake dog-doo, and these great plastic cockroaches you can put in somebody's water glass – ever seen them? You just wind 'em up, and they swim around and kick their little roach legs."

"Wow," says Pete.

"And the eyeballs, of course. That's how me and Mouse got to know each other, right, Mouse? It was kind of like – I don't know, fate or something."

Fate? Ruby heaves a sigh. *Please, oh, please, don't tell us all about it* . . . But Big Skinny – his eyes already misty with memory – is too far gone to notice.

"First day of school, back in – what was it, year four or something? Never saw each other in our lives before this, right, Mouse? And we're sitting there in the canteen, and they're serving this terrible potato salad that day – nowhere near as good as this, Mrs Miller – and old Charlotte Burton leaves hers sitting right across from me while she goes back to get a fork because she had dropped her first one and figured it had lice or something. And I say, 'Man, I wish I had one of them fake eyeballs from Floddenfield's right about now,' and old Mouse – I didn't even *know* him then, like I said – he reaches in his pocket and pulls out *two.* 'Green or purple?' he says. Man, it was beautiful. We've been friends ever since. Right, Mouse?"

Well, anyhow, they live through dinner. And when the last drumstick has disappeared, and the next-to-last photo has been snapped, and Big Skinny has run out of uplifting things to say about vomit and cockroach legs, Mama turns off all the lamps and lights the candles and carries in the shining cake, and they all sing "Happy Birthday" to Pete, who beams through the whole thing and then laughs and covers his ears when Big Skinny tries to put in a little harmony and succeeds only in braying like those half-jackass boys in *Pinocchio*.

"Make a wish, baby," says Mama, and Pete nods and closes his eyes and wishes whatever it is with all his might, and then he blows out his candles in one mighty *whoosh*! And everybody claps.

And finally it's time for the presents: a new mummy book from Ruby (*A Tale of Two Tuts*); a new shirt and a dragon kite and an actual telescope from Mama (just a little one, but the box says it really works); a slightly beat-up-looking remote-control car from Mouse ("It might need a couple of batteries," he explains when it fails to run); and a video of the movie *The Time Machine* from Big Skinny. "That's one kind, anyway," he tells Pete.

"And here's one more," Ed says shyly, handing him the last little package.

"Wow!" says Pete, once he manages to get it open. (Ed must have used up half a roll of tape on the wrapping.) "A new watch!"

"A genuine Olympic-style calibrated sports watch," says Big Skinny, who seems to know a lot more about it than Ed does. "See, champ, it's digital, just like the pros use. It shows *hundredths* of a second – see there? And it's got a stopwatch feature, and it's pressurised and waterproof, so you can wear it when you're deep-sea diving and everything."

"Wow!" Pete says again, strapping it on. "Thanks a lot, Ed."

"Dr Dargan, sweetheart," Mama corrects him.

But Ed says, "Oh, no, please. Ed is fine."

They smile at each other. Again. Then Mama says, "Okay, then, who's ready for cake?"

The words are scarcely out of her mouth when there's another knock at the door.

"Oh, Miss Pierce! How nice – please come in; you're just in time for birthday cake. Is the meeting over already?"

"We left a few minutes early," says Miss Pierce. The "we" includes the parrot, apparently; it's sitting on her shoulder holding a tiny package in its beak. "Go ahead, Lord Byron."

The bird looks blank.

"Oh, for heaven's sake, LB." Miss Pierce strokes the green feathers and whispers something in his ear (or where his ear ought to be, anyway; do birds *have* ears? Ruby wonders. You can't actually see much of anything, but surely –

"SKRRAWKKK!" says Lord Byron, dropping the package and coming to life all at once, ruffling his feathers and stretching his wings. "Happy birthday! Happy birthday!" And then everybody laughs, and Pete runs to pick up the little box, and it turns out to have brown rock inside, which Miss Pierce explains is actually a bit of petrified wood that's about a zillion years old. And Pete's eyes get even wider over that than they did for the watch.

"Wow," he says. "Thanks a lot, Miss Pierce."

"Wonderful," says Mama. "Now, how about that cake?"

"But there's another package on your porch," says Miss Pierce. "Don't you want to open that first?"

Another package? Everyone looks at everyone else — *From you? Not me. Well then, who? Don't ask ME . . .*

But it's there all right, leaning up against the house just beneath the porch light: a fairly large, flat-shaped package, wrapped in plain brown paper, about the size of a Monopoly board, maybe.

"Doesn't seem to be a card," says Ed as he and Mouse and Big Skinny carry the thing inside.

"Maybe it's not ours. Maybe it was delivered here by mistake," Mama begins, but it's too late; Pete is already ripping off the paper.

"Well, look at that, champ; it's some kind of picture —"

"A painting!" says Mama. "A watercolour, I think — well, isn't that nice, Pete? A wonderful watercolour of — of some sort of prehistoric — oh, my goodness, it's . . . it looks just like —"

"Mammook," Pete whispers.

Good grief. What in the world? Ruby blinks in disbelief. She takes off her glasses, rubs off the smudges, puts them on again. Is she seeing things?

But it's Mammook, all right — or a woolly mammoth

that looks just like him, anyway, right down to the button eye and one broken-off tusk. And he's not alone; he's standing beside a box – an old cardboard packing box like the one he disappeared in. Looks like he just stepped out of it, as a matter of fact. Only somehow the box seems to be more than an ordinary box now: there's some sort of magical light coming from it, a kind of golden radiance, swirling up into the air and spilling all over Mammook, too. And the little mammoth is looking up with the happiest, most amazed expression on his face (Ruby doesn't know how the artist got that on there, but there it is), because he's come back, that's what he's done. Not back to the Miller apartment block by the poor old concrete river, but way, way back, to the *real* river, the way it was twenty thousand years ago; a great flashing tumbling splashing blue and white wild water ride of a river, with fish leaping, and beavers swimming, and sun sparkling on the waves, right up to the sandy bank under Mammook's feet. And all around him there are other animals – mammoths like him (is the big one coming towards him his mother?), and giant sloths, and sabre-toothed tigers, and ferocious-looking wolves.

And high, high up in the blue sky above them all, a condor – a great dragon bird – is soaring, with its wings spread so wide, a squirrel in their shadow at straight-up noon might think it was the end of the world . . .

For a moment, nobody says anything. Pete just stands there, looking at the painting. Everybody else just stands there, looking at Pete.

Finally, Big Skinny gives a low whistle. "Whoa. That's some picture, huh, champ?"

Pete doesn't answer. Seems as if he doesn't even hear the question. Ruby can't tell if he likes the picture or hates it. He's studying it so hard, she wouldn't be all that surprised if his eyes burned two perfectly round, blue holes right through it.

"SKRRAWWKK!" says Lord Byron. "Happy birthday! Happy —"

"Shut up," Ruby hisses. *Oh, man, Pete. SAY something . . .* Suddenly she feels sick. He hates it, doesn't he? Well, sure he does; it's breaking his heart. And everybody else knows it too. They're all looking at one another and thinking, *Oh, boy, what genius thought of THIS? Poor kid was having a pretty good birthday, until now . . .*

"Pete?" Mama says gently. "You okay, honey?"

Still Pete doesn't answer. He nods a little, as if he's only half-hearing. Then he picks up the picture and carries it into his room — more of a cubby-hole than a whole room, really; it used to be a little pantry, just off the kitchen.

Ed turns to Mama. He's looking pretty sick himself. "Should we see if he's all right?"

But she shakes her head. "Let's give him a minute," she says. So they all go back to the table, and she starts cutting the cake and handing around slices, but nobody seems very hungry now.

And then a loud banging sound comes from Pete's room, and they all look at one another again: *Oh, boy, he*

REALLY hates it. He's breaking it to pieces. And they get up and hurry to his door —

But Pete hasn't smashed up anything. He was hammering, that's all. And now he's hanging Mammook and his entire old/new world on the wall by his bed, right next to his pillow.

"It's from him," says Pete, his eyes still on the painting. "I guess he heard me make my wish."

Mama sits down beside him. "You mean it's — sort of a message? So we wouldn't be worried about him?"

Pete thinks that over. And then he nods. "He wasn't really lost. He just wanted to go home."

20

It doesn't hit her right away. Not until a whole hour later, when she's washing the party dishes, half-thinking about whether she should wrap up that last little smidgen of cake or just go ahead and eat it, and half-listening to the soft hum of Mama's voice from Pete's room, where she's reading him to sleep. And suddenly there it is, plain as day, blaring in Ruby's brain like a trumpet blast — so clear that her knees go rubbery and she's hot and cold at the same time and has to hold on to the edge of the sink just to keep from falling down.

It was Daddy who painted the picture.

Well, of course it was.

How could she *not* have seen it, even for a second?

She takes a deep breath. Lets it out slowly. It *had* to be him, that's all. Who else could it be? *Come on, Sherlock, look at the evidence*:

Not Mama. No way. Ruby had sort of assumed she was the one, before she really thought about it, but now it's obvious that doesn't make sense. Mama was as surprised as anybody when Pete opened the package.

Ruby's seen her fake this kind of birthday stuff plenty of times, and this was no fake. She's no better at lying than Pete is. Her eyes are always dancing when she's up to something; the more she tries to look innocent, the more the laughter comes bubbling out, blowing her cover.

Definitely not Mama . . .

And definitely not Ed, or his knucklehead protégés. They hardly *know* Pete, for crying out loud. How could they come up with an idea like that? Besides, they all gave him other presents, remember? The watch and *The Time Machine* video and the broken-down remote control car. No way it was any of those guys . . .

Which leaves – who? Miss Pierce? Forget it. The old lady can't paint – she even *said* it once; Ruby remembers it distinctly. It was the first Christmas they lived here, and Miss Pierce was trying to spray a snowman and a Christmas tree on her front window with some of that fake snow that comes in the cans, and making a terrible mess of it. "I'm afraid I'm no artist," she apologised when they found her – practically in tears – wiping it off. So Mama asked if they could help and then bragged about Ruby's artistic ability (which wasn't really much to brag about, although Mama was convinced she was the next Michelangelo or somebody, but at least she could manage a snowman), and Ruby had been in charge of window decorations every since.

No, definitely not Miss Pierce . . .

And definitely not the parrot (he's smart, but not *that* smart) . . .

Leaving only . . .

"Ruby?" Mama comes in so quietly that Ruby jumps a little when she feels the arm around her shoulder. "Thank you, sweetheart."

"Oh. Sure," says Ruby, thinking she means the dishes. "They weren't really all that bad, except for the frying pan. Should I just throw out all this old cooking oil, or did you want to save it?"

"No, I mean – well, thanks for that, too – just leave the rest, honey; I can finish up later. But I was talking about the picture."

"The picture?"

"You know, Pete's present. I thought for a minute there it might be a mistake – when he first opened it, you know, and he looked so – well, you saw his face. But I was wrong; I should have known you understood him better than anybody. He's crazy about it, Ruby. It's just wonderful."

Ruby puts down the glass she's rinsing. She looks at Mama. "It wasn't me."

Mama smiles. "Right. I forgot. It was from Mammook."

"No! I'm not kidding, Mama. I didn't paint that picture. I'm not that good."

"Well, of course you are! I'll never forget those beautiful placemats you made for me that time, and those pretty oven gloves, and that wonderful lolly stick turkey –"

"That was in *nursery school*, Mama! From patterns the teacher gave us. I couldn't draw a woolly mammoth to save my life. I wish I could; I wish I'd thought of it, but I didn't."

"Well, then . . . who?"

Ruby just looks at her. She doesn't say the words: *It was Daddy, don't you see? It had to be Daddy. He's been watching out for us all this time, keeping an eye on us even when we didn't know it. That's how he knew about Mammook; that's how he knew what Pete needed. He hasn't forgotten us, Mama, no matter what you think. He'd have come to the party if he could have. He's still undercover, that's all. He's still working for the CIA or the FBI or some of those other high-priority initials. He's still on his impossible mission or his top-secret stake-out or whatever. Maybe it's too dangerous for him to be seen, that's all; maybe he thinks he'd be putting US in danger. He's got his reasons, Mama, you'll see. He'll explain it all one day. You just have to TRUST him. You just have to have a little FAITH.*

But she doesn't say any of it, not out loud, because what would be the use? She can't prove it. Never mind that she knows it for a fact deep down inside her — that's not the same as proof, and anyway Mama doesn't *want* to hear it; she doesn't *want* to believe it. Ruby could talk herself sick and it wouldn't change Mama's mind about Frankie Miller even the tiniest little bit.

"I don't know, Mama. You tell me."

It's the best Ruby can do. But the truth must have hit Mama, too, even if she's not about to admit it. Because her face changes now. The red creeps across her cheekbones, and her eyes fill up, and she turns away and starts fiddling with the daisies, pulling off leaves that don't really look even the tiniest bit saggy. "Well," she says finally. (Her voice sounds peculiar, as if she's got a bit of a frog in there.) "It was a good party, don't you think? Your friends seemed to enjoy themselves."

Ruby groans. "They're not *my* friends, Mama. It was Pete who invited them."

"Well, I know, but – oh, they're not so bad, really, when you get to know them. Ed says that Vincent's just –"

"Don't tell me. A homicidal maniac with a heart of gold?"

Mama grins. "Well, maybe not homicidal. Anyway, Pete likes him. And he seems to think the world of you."

Ruby looks at her mother suspiciously. Is she teasing her? Did her eyes just sneak a peek out the window at that stupid poem?

But Mama doesn't say another word about it, thank the Lord. And Ruby's got no room in her head to be worrying about Big Skinny Bogart – not tonight of all nights, what with secret messages appearing on her porch and trumpets still blaring in her brain. So she hugs her mum and says, "Great party." And then she goes to bed.

But not to sleep. Not for hours and hours.

No way.

21

CUT TO: A long shot of the earth turning slowly.

Very . . . very . . . slowly.

For the next seven days – on the *outside*, at least – pretty much nothing happens. Nothing, that is, of any interest or importance whatsoever. (You hardly ever have to put up with this sort of thing in films, Ruby notices. Unless your mother is a sucker for subtitles. Or anything set in an English country house. As Pete once said, after watching Mama sob through her tape of *Howards End* for the forty-third time, "I think after I learn Spanish, I'm gonna learn British.")

Well, okay, maybe it is possible that something vaguely interesting is going on *somewhere* on the planet, but the news never makes it to Valleyheart Drive. Mama goes to work, and Pete plays with his presents, and Ruby keeps an eye on him – unless she's busy with the chain gang, like today. In which case Miss Pierce fills in, while Ruby and her fellow convicts spend the morning over on Coldwater in that dried-up drainage ditch with the history mural, wiping splattered egg off Albert Einstein's face.

But all this time, on the *inside*, Ruby is practically full to bursting, because something's coming, she's sure of it, now that they've had this sign from Daddy. It's so close she can almost *taste* it. If only she turns her head just right, if she squints her eyes just so, she'll *see* it, she knows she will: something wonderful, something huge, something that's going to change everything, for ever and ever. Sure, you couldn't show any of this in a film, because she's walking around just like regular, but the world is different now; *she's* different – all charged up, like a jillion-watt bulb. "She's small, but she's wiry," the doctor once said. (It worried her at the time; she had just seen *The Terminator*.) She pictures her insides, whirring and ticking. A tangle of live wires, shooting sparks.

Introducing Ruby ELECTRIC!
Better put on your rubber-soled shoes.
She's got the POWER, man . . .

"Do you think those are circus pigeons?" asks Pete.

"Circus pigeons?" Ruby doesn't have any idea what he's talking about. She hasn't been home but half a minute.

"Over there," says Pete. He's sitting on the porch steps beside Miss Pierce, pointing his new telescope across the street. "Those pigeons over by the river. See 'em?"

Ruby sits down on his other side, looks where he's

looking. A flock of thirty or forty plump little pigeons is lined up neatly along the top of the river wall, just above the oh-so-dreaded red words. Ruby sighs. "Okay, I see 'em. What about 'em?"

"Wait just a second, now . . ." He checks his new watch. "Four, three, two, one — blast-off! Okay, now look!" Pete smiles triumphantly. "See that?"

Ruby nods. Though there's not that much to see, really. The pigeons just take off together, that's all, as if on cue, and go sweeping up into the sky in one great big glorious circle. And then a little while later, they circle back, one after another, and take their places again on top of the wall.

Pretty, sure, but not exactly Barnum and Bailey material.

Pete, however, looks as proud as if he's trained them himself. "Isn't that great?" he says. "They've been doing that every —" He checks his watch again. "Every three point oh-eight minutes for the last half-hour. Haven't they, Miss Pierce?"

Miss Pierce inclines her head gravely. "They have, indeed." She feeds Lord Byron a peanut.

"So what do you think, Ruby? You think they escaped from the circus? Or maybe they got away from some laboratory. Maybe they're *clone* pigeons."

And Ruby says she doesn't know, because she doesn't, of course. But she doesn't really have anywhere special to go, either, so she just sits there peacefully for a bit, letting her mind drift easy, while Pete rambles on about his pigeon theories and wonders how long this has been going on without him ever noticing, and were there pigeons in the Ice Age, and if there were then did that mean their ancestor pigeons had been flying this same circle pattern for twenty thousand years? And all this time, the something that's coming keeps getting closer and closer, and Ruby is trying to picture how it will be, exactly: will their dad just walk up casually, when they're least expecting him? Will he call first? Is he watching them now? If only there were some sign they could give *him* – some signal that would let him know they got his message . . .

"I wish we could fix it back the way it was," says Pete.

"The way what was?" says Ruby. She's only half-listening, because this humongous thing is getting really close now. She could almost *hear* it, if Pete would only hush . . .

"The river. You know, like in my picture. I wish we could make it look like that."

Ruby sits up straight.

Wait a minute.

Wait a minute.

That's not *it*, is it? It couldn't be *that* simple . . .

She looks at Pete. "Say that again?"

"Say what?"

"About the river."

Pete scratches his head, trying to remember it right. "I wish we could make it look like my picture?"

Ohmygosh. Ohmygosh. That IS it, isn't it? The answer . . . the sign . . . the whatever-it-is . . .

And to think that almost *missed* it!

"You okay, Ruby?"

"Hmm?"

"You look kind of funny."

"Oh. No. I'm fine, I'm just . . . Pete, you're a genius, you know that? Isn't he a genius, Miss Pierce?"

Miss Pierce raises and eyebrow. "Very possibly."

Pete gives a modest shrug. "Well, I couldn'ta done it without my telescope. And my new watch."

"Your watch?"

"You know, figured out about the pigeons and everything."

"Not the pigeons; forget the pigeons —"

Pete looks shocked. "Forget the *pigeons*?"

"No, I mean the *wall*, Pete! Don't you get it? The river wall. We could paint it — you know — a whole whaddyacallit . . . a mural! Like the one on Coldwater, with Einstein and everybody —"

"Einstein?" Pete's brow wrinkles. "The guy with the hair?"

Ruby grabs his shoulders. "*Forget* Einstein. I'm talking about your *picture*, Pete! With Mammook and all the mammoths and sabre-toothed tigers and everything. We could paint the river wall just like that, only make it big — make it HUGE, don't you get it?"

"Ohhhh," says Pete. His eyes are enormous. "You mean, so everybody could see?"

"Exactly," says Ruby. "Everybody." *Even* . . . The thought is almost more than she dares finish. It makes her head swim, like a too-sweet soft drink.

Pete shakes his head. "I don't know if I can paint that good."

"That doesn't matter; I can't either. But we have a *pattern*, don't you see? The picture is our pattern! We just follow that; it couldn't be that hard. The art class did it in the hall at school. They took these little designs they'd made on paper and blew 'em up real big with an overhead projector and then traced round 'em and filled 'em in. Only this would be *way* better than that . . ."

Well, of course it would! That was just a bunch of butterflies and bunnies and those dumb smiley faces that were Charlotte Burton's speciality, plus some gross-looking Lizard Guy riding a motorcycle that the boys all loved. But *this* –

"Oh, man, can't you just *see* it?"

Ruby pauses to catch her breath, her heart pounding like thunder in her chest, the vision already complete in her mind's eye, glowing with a golden, unearthly light, shining like the sun itself. She looks at Miss Pierce, who has been sitting here listening quietly all this time, stroking Lord Byron's green neck. "We could do it, couldn't we? Get permission from somebody or – well, doesn't your club do stuff like that? To make the river look nicer? Our group still has thirty-six hours of community service left, and as long as we're painting walls anyway . . ."

Miss Pierce doesn't answer. She nods her head, but slowly, as if she's thinking it over. "It's an idea," she says at last. "A very fine idea. We could talk about it, of course. But oh, my dears, the hornet's nest you'd be stirring up!"

"Hornet's nest?"

"There'd be permits to be gotten, petitions to be signed, miles and miles of red tape . . . Why, you cannot imagine what we went through to get a few dozen trees and a bike path in Long Beach."

"But you got them, right?" asks Ruby.

Miss Pierce smiles. "Oh my, yes. We got them."

"Then we can do this too, can't we? If everybody helps?"

"SKKRRAWWK!" says Lord Bryon, ruffling his feathers. "Help me, Rhonda, help, help me, Rhonda . . ."

Miss Pierce gives him a stern look.

The bird shuts up.

"I know we can do it," says Ruby.

Miss Pierce studies her face for a moment.

The earth turns. Slowly.

And then the old lady winks. "Oh my, yes."

INTERVAL

22

MUSIC UP:

PR-R-UMP-PUM!
PR-R-UM-PA-PA-PUMP-PUM!
PR-R-UM-PA-PA-PUMP-PUM!
PR-R-UM-PA-PA-PUM . . .

FADE IN:

The bank of a mighty river. 20002 BC. A splendid,
sparkling summer afternoon.

In the Ice Age.

They're having a thaw.

                    NARRATOR
    And in the last glorious days of the mighty
    Middle Valley, they would come to call it the
    Season of Signs and Wonders. When the sky

rained secrets, and the river ran wild and free, and the great warrior king came back from the dead at –

"Hey, Miller! This is so cool! Come down here for a minute! You wanna see an eighty-kilo man-eating chicken?"

Ruby sighs, just a little. A patient sort of sigh. Six weeks ago, maybe, an idiotic remark like that might have gotten her goat. But that was then, and this is now, and now . . .

She lifts her paint roller.

Even Big Skinny Bogart can't ruin a day like this.

PR-R-UMP-PUM!

PR-R-UM-PA-PA-PUMP-PUM!

PR-R-UM-PA-PA-PUMP-PUM!

PR-R-UM-PA-PA- –

"Never mind, Miller! I swear, you're gonna love this. Just hang on, okay? I'll bring it up!"

Great. He's bringing it up. Oh well, if it'll make him happy. As long as he doesn't waste *too* much time. They're just getting *started* here, for heaven's sake; they've barely even begun to begin. And there's still such an awful lot to do . . .

Ruby looks down – way, way down – from her chosen perch on the top floor of the scaffolding, which by now covers a good five hundred square feet of the river wall. From here, beside Big Skinny, on assorted levels below

her, she can see Mama and Pete and Ed and Miss Pierce
and Mouse and the River Authority Supervisor and
sour-faced Theo and a couple of the old chain gang, plus
at least a dozen volunteers from the Friends of the Los
Angeles River, all working away –

As the mighty mural emerges, bit by bit.

PR-R-UM-PA-PA-PUM!

Not that all of this has happened overnight, exactly.
It's been a while since that day on the porch with Pete
and the pigeons. Six weeks, right?

The longest six weeks in the entire history of the
world.

That's how it felt to Ruby, anyway, hours and hours
(and not just her thirty-six leftover community-service
hours, either – *that* turned out to be the joke of the
century) and then more hours and days and weeks and
even *months* – well, a month and a half, anyway; they're
in the middle of August now. And Miss Pierce says
that's quick for a project like this, some kind of world
record or something, especially since everything she said
would happen has happened, three times over: red tape
for miles, for *millennia*, it seemed to Ruby.

Of course if this was a film, she could have just
crammed the whole thing into a stirring two-minute
musical montage and been done with it. That would
have been infinitely more efficient than the real-life
version, which was about as stirring as watching hair
grow. First they had to wait for the Friends of the Los

Angeles River to meet. There was a whole week gone, right off the bat. And when they all finally got to the meeting – Miss Pierce had invited Ruby and Pete to come along, picture in hand, to argue their case, and naturally Mama and Ed were there, too, and as if that weren't already plenty, Ed had brought Big Skinny and Mouse along besides (to broaden their sense of civic responsibility, Ruby supposed, although she could have told him *that* was a big fat waste of time) – even then, the mural proposal wasn't the first order of business. Or the second. Or the third, fourth, or fifth. Turned out the Friends had bigger things on their minds – bigger than woolly mammoths even. According to Miss Pierce, their long-term goal was to dig up every last unnecessary inch of concrete from the waterway and make it a *real* river again. But of course that was going to take fifty years or something and who knew how many elections and acts of Parliament and no telling what all. And meanwhile the Friends were just doing whatever they could to ease the poor old river's pain, a little at a time: petitioning the county for more parks and fewer car parks (to soften its hard edges, Miss Pierce explained), working with wildlife conservancies and environmental agencies (filing bird migration reports was Miss Pierce's speciality), bringing lawsuits against industrial polluters and would-be developers ("and of course the county itself, on occasion," Miss Pierce told them, "when the powers that be start backsliding towards muddle-headedness"). The list went on and on. Ruby just sat there, listening, for more than an hour, feeling smaller and sillier by the second. Why on earth had she come? The *mayor* was here, for crying out loud. There were *film stars* in the audience. She was almost positive that was the guy who morphed into an alien truck driver on that last episode of *Roswell*, sitting right there in the third row. She couldn't do it, that's all – not with her heart pounding like this, her throat dry as dust – no way she could stand up in front of all these important people and explain about – about what? Mammook? How she wanted to cover up the graffiti on the river wall with a giant picture of her little brother's moth-eaten *puppet*? They would laugh themselves cross-eyed, that's what they would do. They would poke each other and whisper snide remarks and –

"Ruby and Pete Miller," she heard Miss Pierce say into the microphone just then, "P" popping, spit flying, sound bouncing around the meeting hall like the voice of doom, "two young neighbours of yours and mine who are with us tonight, bringing with them a very interesting proposition."

Trapped.

For a second Ruby just sat there, frozen, her tongue stuck to the roof of her mouth like a useless lump of putty . . .

And then she saw Mouse looking at her, clearly hoping she'd mess up, and Big Skinny looking at her, nodding like a dope, and Mama and Ed looking at her, smiling encouragingly.

Not that any one of these was any big deal by itself. But added all together – well, they added up, that's all.

And here was the kicker: in her worry for her daughter (when she saw the panic in Ruby's eyes), Mama had grabbed Ed's hand. Maybe – probably – without even knowing it.

Still.

Suddenly Ruby was herself again. Totally defrosted. Suddenly she just couldn't *wait* to get up to that podium.

Besides, Pete was halfway there already, lugging the painting.

It wasn't so bad, really, once she started talking. She'd written out her speech ahead of time, thank goodness; she'd watched the Oscars enough times to be fully aware of the perils of spontaneity. And overall she thought it went pretty well, although she was a little surprised when people laughed in some of the most serious places. (They must have misunderstood her, was all. Okay, sure, when she talked about "neighbourhoods panting for the picturesque like river rats in a drought," it did sort of sound like "river routs in a drat". But come on. There wasn't anything the least bit funny about "the glaring need to rise up, to wake from this hellish nightmare and toil ever onward towards the light at the end of the long, dark, graffiti-infested tunnel".)

Anyhow they clapped when she was done. That was a relief. Somebody – Ruby hoped it wasn't Ed, but she had her suspicions – even yelled, "Bravo!" And somebody else whistled one of those mortifyingly loud, eardrum-smashing, headache-making whistles. (Somebody, shoot; it was Big Skinny, no question about it.) And then Miss

Pierce asked a guy in the back to turn off the lights, and she flipped on the overhead projector – Ruby had told her about the art class's bunnies and Lizard Man – and she put on the transparency they had made from Pete's picture. And when the image rose, shining, on the giant screen at the back of the meeting hall . . .

The audience gasped.

They actually *gasped*.

The sound gave Ruby goose bumps clear up to the top of her skull.

Yes! She told herself. *We've got 'em now, for sure . . .*

"Who's the artist?" the alien truck driver shouted out.

She should have been ready for that, but she wasn't. It hadn't even occurred to her that anybody might ask a question like that. Her mind began to race. What was she supposed to say? There was Pete, staring right at her. She knew what *his* answer would be, but that didn't help any. She didn't want to burst his bubble, but she couldn't very well tell the mayor and them that *Mammook* had painted the picture. And as for the truth . . . well, she didn't have any more proof now than she had the night of the birthday party, but that didn't change a thing; she was still positive her dad had his reasons for keeping his gift a secret. It might jeopardise his whole mission if anybody knew he'd been in the area; no way he could take a chance on having his identity revealed before he was absolutely ready. So obviously he couldn't just . . . just . . .

"He wishes to remain anonymous," said Miss Pierce.

Thank God.

Ruby recommenced breathing.

Pete whispered something to Miss Pierce. She nodded, then picked up the microphone again: "He's shy."

By which Pete meant Mammook, of course, though only six other people in the building actually understood. But there just wasn't any way to explain it any better, and fortunately the alien truck driver seemed satisfied. And as for everybody else – well, that gasp had pretty much sealed the deal.

Not that this one meeting was the end of the battle. Not by a long shot. The Friends still had to talk to the River Authority and the River Authority had to talk to the Town Hall and the Town Hall had to talk to the Official Head of the newly appointed Subcommittee of the Office in Charge of Neighbourhood-Sponsored Murals (or whatever it was called), and on and on and on. For a while there Ruby was afraid they never *would* shut up.

But that's all behind them now. All that matters on this shining summer day is that it's happening. It's really happening. They've got a long, long way to go, sure, but this is the fun part – the magic part – the part where every morning she wakes up and can't wait to get back to it, to be working, bringing it to life: that grand, glorious, golden picture she can still see so clearly in her mind. Even if it's just a tiny bit at a time some days, even if –

"Okay, Miller, I got it! Here's the man-eating chicken! You ready?"

Ruby comes back to earth with a thud, just in time to see Big Skinny's long legs clambering up the scaffolding. Oh well. Things could be worse. He is helping, after all. He and Mouse are done with their required hours, too; they don't have to be here now, any more than Ruby does. She thought for sure they'd be long gone before this and back to their regular routine. (Bound to be hundreds more old ladies out there dying to be mooned.) But for some reason the crazy guys keep showing up here at the river, day after day. And working – actually *working*; that's what Ruby can't get over. Turns out they have a real knack for this kind of thing.

All of which ought to make her grateful, she supposes. Or at least, less inclined to gag every time they breathe in her direction.

But then nobody said it would be *easy*.

She sighs again and rolls a broad stroke of blue across the Ice Age sky. "As ready as I'll ever be, I guess."

Big Skinny grins and swings himself the rest of the way up. There's a smear of bright orange paint on his left cheek (the colour of the prehistoric poppies), a bit of twenty-thousand-year-old ivy green matted in his hair. "Okay, now close your eyes. Don't be scared. You're not scared, are you? Here it comes: an eighty-kilo man-eating chicken. Ready, set – TA-DA!"

Ruby opens her eyes.

Oh, for crying out loud.

It's a snapshot of Ed at Pete's party, biting into a drumstick.

"Get it?" Big Skinny waves the photo over his head

162

like a victory flag. He's so tickled, he can barely get the words out. "An eighty-kilo man . . . eating *chicken*!"

Ruby doesn't *mean* to laugh. It just takes her by surprise, is the thing. Ordinarily she wouldn't dream of laughing at such a dumb joke – at *any* of Big Skinny's dumb jokes – but she wasn't ready for this one, that's all. The chuckle slips out of her before she can stop it. And of course he's laughing, too; they're both laughing. *Everybody's* laughing – even Ed himself. The whole scaffolding is shaking, they're all laughing so hard at the dumbest joke there ever was.

And in the last glorious days of the mighty Middle Valley, they would come to call it the Season of Signs and Wonders . . .

"Who's up for pizza?" asks Ed, beaming pinkly.

Ruby turns back to her blue sky. "No, thanks."

But she's overruled by a dozen voices. For now, at least, the wall will have to wait.

"Don't worry," says Big Skinny. "It'll still be here tomorrow."

And it will.

Things could definitely be worse.

23

Dear Mr Spielberg:

~~My name is Ruby Miller. I am a student an honour student at Rutherford B. Hayes Middle a future filmmaker You don't know me, however We have not as yet actually met but I hope that soon I might speedily rectify this unfortunate this circumstantial this abysmal state of~~

Dear Mr Spielberg:

~~Thank you in advance for making time in what I realise must be a vastly overcrowded~~

Dear Mr Spielberg:

Let me begin by saying that I have seen all your films, and thoroughly enjoyed the vast majority. I myself am especially ~~admiring of impressed by~~ smitten with the social conscientiousness of your more serious efforts, but I hasten to add that along with my younger

brother (Peter Miller), I am also an
enthusiastic fan of all those that are in any way
futuristic, ancient tomb-related, or dealing with
dinosaurs.

~~But no doubt you have heard all this before,
so let me get to the~~

~~What are you doing next~~

~~If you happen to be free on~~

I would like to take this opportunity, Mr
Spielberg, to personally invite you to what
promises to be an exciting and fun-filled
afternoon in the heart of the San Fernando
Valley. Perchance you are already familiar
with the effort that ~~has of late is currently~~
even as I pen these words is forging a new
milestone in the beautification of our beloved
community?

I am referring (as you've ~~probably~~ no doubt
guessed) to the ~~new~~ totally all-new
neighbourhood produced mural that will be
unveiled on a portion of the wall of the Los
Angeles River on the upcoming holiday in
honour of our great nation's workforce,
Monday, September 2nd (Labour Day ~~to the
common man to meet~~ in common parlance,
but also known henceforth on this very
special occasion as Dedication Day), just a
scant two weeks from now, when the
culmination of the heroic efforts of many will
at long last ~~reach total completion result in~~

~~fruition~~ be finished. There will be balloons,
prizes (including a delicious dinner for 2 at
Deano's Pizzeria), free entertainment (plans
are apace for a possible parrot and puppet
show, as well as an inspirational poetry
reading by Miss Angela Pierce), and, of course,
fun for the entire family. So please, Mr
Spielberg, feel free to bring the whole gang! (I
am enclosing a flyer with further information,
as well as a map and parking suggestions, for
your convenience.)

~~You will also no doubt have noted by now~~
~~In addition to~~
~~One more thing, Mr S~~

I am also enclosing one additional item that
I hope you will find time to peruse at your
leisure: a copy of the first act (7 pages) of my
latest screenplay, currently titled ~~SHE KNEW~~
~~NOT FEAR THE MAMMOTH WEEPS BLOODY~~
~~MOON IN~~ BITTER WERE THE BONES, which
(as it was inspired by the very heroic mural in
question) I thought you might find to be of
particular interest.

~~And finally~~
~~With no further ado~~

In closing, Mr Spielberg, let me say that it
has been a pleasure writing to you, and that I
wish you the very best of luck with all that
remains of your career. I sincerely hope that in
the near future we might find ourselves

~~collabor colabbor~~ colaboratting on many fine
cinematic endeavours.

> Respectfully yours,
> Ruby Miller

There. That ought to do it.

Ruby puts down the pile of crossed-out and corrected
pages on her bedside table. Takes off her glasses. Climbs
under the covers. Switches off the light.

Lies there with her eyes wide open, listening to
herself breathe.

She'll have to type it out again first thing in the
morning, of course. It has to be perfect when he reads it.
She shivers a little, picturing the scene. How he'll walk
to the front door, and flip through all his post – piles of
ordinary fan letters, naturally, and all his regular
correspondence (thank-you notes from Julia and Tom, a
birthday greeting from Denzel, another invitation to the
Governor's Ball. The usual). And then he'll come to
Ruby's letter – she'll have borrowed one of the Friends'
envelopes, so it'll look official – and okay, sure, maybe
he'll think for a second, *Oh, just another boring civic
occasion*. But he'll keep on reading, because he's
extremely civic-minded. Everybody knows that. And
he'll start thinking, *Well, this certainly does sound like a
good cause. Maybe we'll just swing by for an hour or two* . . .

And then he'll see her screenplay.

Well, the first seven pages, at least. It would have
been nice if she'd had time to finish it, but she had to be

realistic. What with her days filled up with the painting and all, the script might take her another week or maybe even two, and she can't wait until *then* to invite Mr Spielberg. She has to give him time to make his plans.

Besides, all the books say the first ten pages are the most important when you're selling a film, because producers hate to read and they hardly ever get any further than that anyway. So she figures she'll just give him a taste now, to get him interested – seven is *practically* ten – and then when she meets him in person she can sum up the rest: how Winona the Warrior Princess sets out on her perilous quest (after her brave father the king is killed by evil-doers, and her mother the queen dies tragically in the Great Avalanche), and all the various unspeakable dangers she has to face, and how she ultimately overcomes everything, thereby rescuing the king (who was never *really* dead) from the curse of the time-travelling psychopath, Malachai the Malevolent.

How could he *not* love a story like that?

It's really weird, too, how the whole thing came to her. It was like another sign or something, an actual *omen* this time. It gives her the chills all over again, just thinking about it. It was just before lunch today, while she was in the middle of putting the second coat of black paint on the condor's wings (they use this special formula that's supposed to be waterproof and weather-proof and never-peeling, for which Ruby is particularly grateful, since the condor happens to be flying directly over the spot on the wall where those embarrassing red words used to be). And meanwhile Miss Pierce was telling them all this amazing stuff about *real* California condors – how unbelievably huge they are, and how they're almost totally extinct, and how the zoo is trying to rescue them and breed them in captivity and raise a bunch of new ones, and then set them free in the mountains again.

Only the problem is, sometimes the condor mothers don't know how they're supposed to act in cages. They get so used to having all their food brought to them, they forget how to feed their own babies. And then of course the babies don't have a clue when *they* grow up. So for a while it was just a big mess, and nobody knew what to do. But then the zoo workers thought of this great trick: they started wearing condor masks at feeding time, and condor puppet claws on their hands, so the chicks wouldn't realise they were getting their food from humans. And the workers can't be one bit nice to them either – at least, not when they're in their regular uniforms. Sometimes they have to rush towards the young condors and make horrible noises and even turn them upside down, so they'll learn to be afraid of all people. Otherwise, when they're set free, they might get homesick for the zoo and try to fly back to town, where they could get tangled in electric wires and phone lines and probably be killed.

Of course it still *sounds* cruel. Pete hated the idea. "They *have* to scare 'em?" he asked Miss Pierce. But she said the workers are saving their lives, really. They figure if the babies are frightened enough, they'll want to stay up in the mountains, where they'll be safe.

So anyhow, she had just told them all that, and Ruby was thinking it over while she painted the wings, and imagining how it would feel inside a condor mask (they're just not all that attractive, face-wise, except to other condors). Plus — somewhere in the back of her mind — her new story was still bouncing around: what, exactly, was the nature of the king's curse? Was he deep-frozen, possibly, in the space-time continuum? Or stricken with supernatural shrinkage? It would work either way; the main thing was he'd been gone so long from his icy kingdom that everybody figured he was dead. But it still felt like Ruby was *missing* something. Unless . . .

Her painting hand trembled . . .

Unless the real truth was even *more* unspeakable:

WINONA

Transformed? What are thou saying, O wise and ancient crone? The king is transformed? O horror! Into what foul beast?

ANCIENT CRONE

Not so foul, my child. Not the sort of foul thou thinkest. Lift up thine eyes to yon heavens. What doest thou see?

WINONA

Why, nothing. O withered one, naught but yon condor, flying bold and free in the great blue dome of —

(a hideous pause, as the full calamitous import
of the dread revelation turns her brave young
blood to coldest ice)
Oh, no!

ANCIENT CRONE
Courage, Princess.

WINONA
Thou meant FOWL?

ANCIENT CRONE
Where there's life, there's hope. Yet cometh a
dark cloud attached to this silver lining. 'Tis
true, the king lives, but – oh, lady, I am loath
to say it -

WINONA
(with a deathly pallor)
He's a bird.

And right then – right that very second, when these
very words were tumbling around inside Ruby's head –
a shadow passed across the sun, and she looked up from
the wall to see what it was (it couldn't be an actual
raincloud in the middle of August) . . .
And there was the biggest bird she'd ever seen,
soaring high above her, so high she couldn't even tell
what colour it was at first. So then she shaded her eyes
and looked and looked, and she saw that the wings were

black and white – *black and white*, no kidding – just like the ones she was painting. And even though it had to be thirty degrees at least, ice ran up and down her spine.

"A condor!" she shouted. "Look at that! Look, everybody! Do you see?"

"Where?" Big Skinny shouted back.

"Right *there*!" said Ruby, pointing to the sky.

And then they *all* shaded their eyes and stood there together looking, and it was a magical moment, just like in a film . . .

Until –

"That ain't any condor. That's just an old turkey buzzard," said Mouse.

Okay, so it turned out he was right. Technically. Although the correct term was turkey *vulture*, not buzzard. When they went home, Miss Pierce showed Ruby and Pete the pictures in her bird book. It wasn't a condor, that much was clear. The black and white underwing pattern was different after all (Ruby should have seen that right away), and its wingspan wasn't even two yards, peanuts to the condor's three. Still, it was definitely in the same ball park – just a couple of cousins removed, maybe – with its terrifying talons, and long, graceful flight, and a beak only a mother vulture could love.

And the real thing was still out there *somewhere*, right? One of these days, she'd see it.

"Hope is the thing with feathers," said Miss Pierce.

Pete cocked his head a little to one side. He was still studying the picture. "If you took off the feathers, it would look just like the pterodactyls in *Jurassic Park*."

He really is a genius.

Ruby almost had to go lie down.

Because that's when it hit her, deep within her electric insides. She could feel her brain sizzling; she could practically smell the smoke. Come on. This was no coincidence. Two omens in a single day? It was all *connected* in some vast, mysterious pattern: condors, pterodactyls, Spielberg! It was all meant to be!

Which is why she spent the rest of the day holed up in her room, typing her fingers to the bone. Shaping up those first seven pages and sweating over her letter. And why she's lying here in bed now, wide awake still, picturing those vulture wings just over a yard wider –

When she hears the phone ring, and her mother's voice, answering.

And then a pause. "Hello, Frankie."

24

SMASH CUT:

A run-down apartment building. Early the next morning.

MOVE IN with the sun through a gap in the mini-blinds, hanging crookedly in a window. It creeps through the room, touching its contents, one after another: an old yellow chest of drawers plastered with baseball stickers. A stray sock. A cap with a plastic turtle on top. One ukulele (stringless). A fake safety pin (to be worn in the nose). Two autographed posters: John Wayne and Yosemite Sam. Last of all the light settles on a bed, with a large teenager in it. He's still deep in some dream, apparently; you can see his eyeballs following the action behind the lids.

He smiles a little. Chuckles softly. Then twitches a bit as the sun hits him squarely in the face.

The clock on the bedside table makes a small click. 7.00.

"*Vincent! Buon giorno!*" a rusty voice calls. "Up, up, up, Vincente! You hear me, no? *Svegli!*"

Big Skinny opens his eyes. "I'm awake, Nonna!"

It's the same every morning. At seven on the nose, school or no school, his grandmother comes shuffling down the hall (she's little, but she's wide, with bad knees and bunions) wearing her old blue bathrobe and the slippers with the torn elastic band. *"Buon giorno, Vincente!* Up, up, up! It's seven o'clock!"

"I'm awake, Nonna!" he calls again now, just like always. But of course she doesn't hear him. She never puts in her hearing aid this early.

So Big Skinny yawns, and stretches, and scratches his belly, and lies there waiting for her to come check him. What was it he was dreaming – something really funny, right? Oh, yeah. He and Mouse had found a whole box full of those great little super-bouncy balls and given it to Miller to open, and they went bouncing all over the place, and she laughed and laughed . . .

Nonna pushes his door wide and comes shuffling in. "Up, up, up!" she says, clapping her hands. She leans in close to see if he's paying attention. Her breath smells like Christmas trees. Always a good sign. She must have remembered to soak her teeth. "Vincente! *Rapidamente!* It's seven o'clock!"

Big Skinny grins up into the solemn old face. *"Buon giorno, Nonna."*

"Buon giorno," says Nonna. *"Mio bello ragazzo."* She smoothes his pillow-mussed hair. "My beautiful boy." Then she straightens and gives him a firm little rap on the shoulder. "Up, up, up! *Il caffè è caldo."*

She shuffles out again.

Big Skinny stretches contentedly.

Buon giorno, Vincente.

It's a whole new day.

He's scarcely finished his excellent coffee and six pieces of only slightly burned toast (Nonna is in charge of the *caffè*; he's the cook), when he sees Ed and Mouse pulling up in the car park outside. Big Skinny and Mouse don't ordinarily need a ride to the river; most days they just go over there on their boards. But Ed asked them yesterday if they could give him a hand this morning hauling the last load of supplies – super-size paint cans and whatnot – from the hardware store. So here he is now, at the door with Mouse, and here's Nonna, smiling and nodding from her chair by the television. She's nuts about old Ed, even though she hardly ever hears a word he's saying.

"*Buon giorno, buon giorno, Dottore e Matthew!* Sit! Sit! You will have *caffè*, no?"

"No, no," says Ed. "Thank you, Mrs Bogart. I just had a cup, and –"

"Sit, sit, sit! Vincente, more *caffè*!"

Ed sits. Mouse too. Big Skinny brings the coffee. And then they all just sit there, sipping and swallowing, while Ed does his best to make conversation.

"So how have you been feeling, Mrs Bogart? You're certainly looking well."

Nonna puts her hand to her right ear. "*Scusi?*"

Ed tries again. "I SAID, YOU'RE CERTAINLY LOOKING WELL."

"*Bella, Nonna,*" says Big Skinny.

"*Grazie*," says Nonna, nodding. "Maybe it will rain."

"Rain?" Ed looks surprised.

"*Forse*," says Nonna.

"Maybe," Big Skinny explains.

Nonna points at the television. "They show on the Weather Channel. *S'il vento* — how you say, Vincente?"

"The wind."

"*Si.* The wind. *En il Pacifico.* If he change."

Mouse shakes his head. "It never rains in August."

"*Forse*," says Nonna. "Big wind. *Molto grande.*" She sighs and pulls herself out of her chair. "Better take *un ombrello.*" She shuffles over to the coat cupboard and roots around for a while. Returns finally with one of those pink see-through plastic things shaped like an upside-down tulip.

So Big Skinny takes it, just to make her happy. Even though he can't help feeling sort of silly. This is definitely a girl's model; he can see Mouse smirking already. Plus there's not a single cloud in the whole sky.

Not a breath of *il vento* either; he and Mouse are both sweating by the time they're done at the hardware store. "You think we really need all this paint?" Big Skinny asks as they push their loaded trolleys out to Ed's car. "I thought we were almost finished."

"One more coat," says Ed. "That's what the experts tell me. Better to be on the safe side, I guess." He reaches in his jacket pocket for his keys (he always wears his Chiropody Centre windbreaker to paint in, even when it's hot as blazes). "And then when that dries, we'll be pretty much —" He stops in his tracks. "Oh dear. Oh, my goodness . . ." He's gone all red in the face. Now he's searching through *all* his pockets.

"Ed?" Big Skinny taps him on the back. "You've got your keys right there in your hand."

"No, no, not keys, where's my — did either of you see a — a little box with a — it's wrapped in — in sort of goldish . . . Oh, never mind, here it is."

Big Skinny cocks an eyebrow. "Everything okay?"

"Oh, yes. Sure. I just thought for a minute —" Ed stops again. His eyes go to Mouse. Not that he means anything by it, Big Skinny knows that. But old Mouse, he's always sort of grouchy about getting blamed for everything.

"You thought I took it?" He's already scowling.

"No, no. I just —"

"Sure you did. You thought I took it."

Ed's face is about the colour of his rear lights now. But at least he's not like some old guys. He knows how to admit when he's wrong. "I'm sorry, Matthew. It was only for a second."

"Why would I take some stupid little box?"

Ed puts a hand on his shoulder. "No reason. None at all. I don't know what I was thinking. It's my own fault; I shouldn't have even brought this with me today. I only — well, I've been waiting for the right moment, but I wasn't sure if that would . . . I mean, you never know, do you, when the opportunity might —"

"Ed!" Big Skinny shouts, as it comes to him all in a flash. "That box — there wouldn't be a *ring* in it, would there?"

Ed doesn't say a word. Looks like he can't. Also looks like he's trying not to smile too big. He just stands there all red-faced, staring at that little gold package.

"I knew it! There *is* a ring in there! How 'bout that, Mouse? Old Ed's gonna ask Miller's mum to be Mrs Ed! Shoot, you can't blame him for being worried. Little box like that don't come from the supermarket. Am I right?" Big Skinny pounds Ed on the back. "Congratulations, man! Way to go!"

But old Ed shakes his head and lifts his hands in a pipe-down signal. "No, please, you can't mention this to anybody . . ." He looks all around, like he's checking for car-park spies. "There's nothing definite. I haven't even asked her yet. She might say no."

Big Skinny gives his back another slap. "Aw, come on, Ed, are you kidding me? How could she say no to a guy like you? You're the man, man! You're the *best*! She's gonna snap you up!"

Ed smiles. "I appreciate the vote of confidence. But if you don't mind, let's just keep this to ourselves for now. Okay?"

"Absolutely, Ed. We're cool with that. We ain't gonna breathe a word. It's probably better if you ask her personally. Right, Mouse?"

Mouse was still a little sore. He takes him time answering. But finally he shrugs. "Yeah, right. Whatever."

So that's it, then; they're sworn to secrecy. But Big Skinny grins all the way to the river. Oh, man, he'd give anything to see Miller's face when she hears. Girls love weddings. He wonders if she'll let on how excited she is. He's noticed she's kind of funny that way, not saying all that much about everything that's going on in that head of hers. But you can always tell if she's happy by this lit-up look she gets – when she's working on the wall, say, or when something makes her laugh. It's like bonfires are burning up inside her. You could almost toast marshmallows.

Of course, when she's *not* happy – well, that's even easier to tell. You don't have to be a superbrain like her to figure *that* out.

But she's been in a lot better mood in general lately, and this news ought to be the icing on the cake. The wedding cake, right? Big Skinny chuckles. Icing on the wedding cake, that's pretty good . . .

Still, a promise is a promise. Fun'll have to wait for now. But maybe not for too long, by the look of it. Shoot, if anybody's going to give anything away, it'll probably be Ed himself. You never saw a person with a face so full of a secret. By the time they get to the wall and see the Millers coming down by the bridge, he seems pretty near bursting with it. Big Skinny has to practically hold his own jaws shut with both hands just to keep from laughing out loud.

But then the family comes closer, and he takes one look at *Miller's* face, and her mum's face, and the little champ's face . . .

And he sees right away: this might not be old Ed's day after all.

"Beautiful morning," says Ed.

"Beautiful," says Mrs M. She doesn't sound too excited about it. Usually she's got a smile for everybody. But now she glances towards her kids and gives Ed one of those private-code looks old people are always giving each other (for some reason they think nobody else can see 'em): *It ain't all THAT beautiful; actually we're wading in it but I can't talk now.*

"What are *you* staring at?" Miller's voice makes Big Skinny jump, just a little. He's been studying Ed and Mrs M so hard, he's sort of lost track of her for a second.

"Hey, Miller." No sense saying he wasn't staring. "Everything all right?"

"Yeah, sure," she mutters, not really looking at him. Just brushes past and reaches into the boot of Ed's car for a new paint roller. "Why wouldn't it be?"

"I don't know, I just – well, it seemed like you were in such a good mood yesterday."

She swings around, glaring. "I'm still in a good mood. I'm in a *great* mood, okay? We just have a lot of work to do, that's all."

"Okay, okay. Sorry."

"I just don't have time to be standing around, that's all."

She stomps off towards the scaffolding.

"Man," stays Mouse. "Who broke *her* broomstick?"

Big Skinny lifts a warning finger. "I'm not gonna tell you again, Mouse. Don't talk about Miller that way."

"Okay, okay. Jeez. A person can't open his mouth around here. What's wrong with everybody today?"

Big Skinny doesn't have a clue. But there's *something* weird in the air, that's for sure. And it just keeps on getting weirder, though it's hard to say why. Nobody's talking much about anything, really. Even when the other volunteers from the Friends get there, it's nothing but dogs and diets and the price of petrol in West Covina. And the whole time old Miller never makes a peep. She's just over there slapping paint on the wall like it's somebody she knows and don't care much for, and looking *dark*, man, like maybe *she's* that big storm Nonna saw on the Weather Channel; like thunder and lightning might start shooting out of her any second.

Of course Big Skinny's seen her mad before. But this is more than mad. Heavier somehow. He can almost see whatever it is, sitting there on her shoulders. Plus her glasses keep going foggy on her. It just bothers him, that's all. He can't stand to see her looking so steamed up and weighed down, both at once.

"Hey, champ," he says to Pete, first chance he gets. The two of them are over near the bridge by the drinks cooler, taking a break. "Is there something wrong with Mill — with your sister?"

"Yep," says Pete. He's having a kind of a hard time with the pull tab on the top of his Coke.

"Here, let me get that for you. These things are a pain, aren't they?"

"Yep," says Pete.

Big Skinny waits for him to go on.

He doesn't.

"So what is it that's bothering her?"

Pete scratches a mosquito bite. "Our daddy called last night."

"Your dad?" Big Skinny thinks that over. He's never met their dad, right? Although he sort of *almost* did, if you count that time he thought he was chasing him at the park. "What'd he say?"

"He wanted us to meet him for dinner."

"Oh." Another pause. "So . . . are you going?"

Pete shakes his head.

"Why not?"

"Mama said no."

"Just . . . no?"

Pete scrunches up his eyebrows, thinking back. "She said, 'No, not again. Not this time. Enough is enough.'"

Oh.

So that's how it is.

The dad's one of those guys. *Poor old Miller . . .*

Big Skinny just sits there.

Well, what are you gonna do?

He looks at Pete. "You're okay, though, right, champ?"

Pete stares down at his Coke. He seems a little embarrassed. "I don't remember him too good."

"Oh." Big Skinny nods. "But you can't help that, right? Listen, don't sweat it. I don't remember mine, either."

Pete looks up. "You don't?"

"Well, you know. Just a couple of things." Big Skinny hasn't thought about it in a while. There was that one day at the baseball practice — he can hear that more than see it: *Level it out, son! Just meet the ball, don't kill it!* He couldn't have been more than four. And the Hallowe'en with the werewolf — *Aw, come on, Vinnie. It's only your papa, don't cry.* That's pretty much it, though. Not enough to really add up to anything. And he's not altogether sure of the werewolf part; that might have been a dream.

He's quiet for a moment. The champ looks kind of down. Big Skinny gives him a fake punch on the shoulder. "But now we got Ed, right?"

"Ed?"

Big Skinny grins. The thought of that little gold box cheers him right up. He points at the wall below. From here the river curves a little, so you can just see old Ed in the middle of the scaffolding, somewhere around the giant sloth level. Looks like he's trying to paint and listen to Miller's mum on his left, while that actor guy from *Roswell* is talking to him on his right. He's hopping on one foot and holding up the other one to show Ed where it hurts.

Pete watches for a minute of two. He seems kind of undecided. "You think he can yo-yo?"

"Who, Ed?"

Pete nods.

Good question. Big Skinny never really thought about it before. "I don't know," he says. "Maybe we should ask him."

So they finish their drinks and start heading back that way. Big Skinny's feeling a lot better now that he understands everything. *Poor old Miller . . .* He can still see her down there, working up a storm. And Mouse right there matching her, paint slap for paint slap. Funny, Big Skinny never noticed before – they're exactly the same size. But then they're alike in a lot of ways, when you think about it. They just got off on the wrong foot, that's all. He hopes old Ed won't wait too long to give Mrs M the ring. That way everybody can start feeling better. Maybe on their lunch break. It must be nearly noon. They could go somewhere nice, like Hamburger Hamlet.

"You got the time, Champ?"

Pete holds up his wrist: eleven forty-eight, exactly.

"Thanks," says Big Skinny. His stomach rumbles. *Icing on the wedding cake. Suggest chocolate.*

It's eleven forty-eight point two when the yelling starts.

25

"*Blue!*"

"*Gold!*"

They're *blue*, you moron!"

"Who you calling a moron?"

"Who do you think?"

"Hey, guys!"

Ruby looks up. Oh, great. Just what she needed. Here's the other half of the Dead-End Duo, back from his break, clambering down the scaffolding with Pete.

"So how's it going?" Big Skinny grins cluelessly. "Everybody happy?"

Ruby clenches her teeth and ignores him. One idiot at a time. It's Mouse she wants to murder at the moment. "*Blue,*" she says again, shaking her paint roller in his face. "Who said you could change 'em, anyway?"

"I did, okay? Me, the moron. A condor's eyes are *gold*, not blue."

It's all Ruby can do just to keep from choking him. "I'm not telling you again, Mouse. Leave 'em alone."

"You don't believe me? Go look it up. It's in the encyclopedia."

"Well, there you go," says Big Skinny, patting both their shoulders. "We'll just run over to the library and —"

"I don't *need* to look it up," Ruby jerks away so violently, the whole scaffolding wobbles. They all grab hold of the railing to keep from pitching right over. "I don't *care* about the encyclopedia. They're blue in Pete's picture. Right, Pete? That's our *pattern*, okay? That's how the painter wanted it."

Mouse sneers. "How do *you* know what he wanted? Maybe he made a mistake — you ever think of that? Maybe he got it wrong. Big deal. That don't mean we have to *keep* it wrong."

"It does if I say so."

"Oh, year? Who crowned *you* queen?"

"Everything okay up there?" It's Ed, calling from the level below.

"Oh, sure, Ed, everything's fine!" Big Skinny calls back. "We're fine, right, guys? Come on now — blue, gold — it don't really matter, does it? Maybe you could do one of each. How 'bout that?"

Ruby just stares at him. She's surrounded by nitwits. And now Ed and Mama are climbing up — the last two people in the world she wants to hang around with today. (They might not realise it yet, but she's not speaking to either of them.) Meanwhile, Miss Pierce and all the others are craning *their* necks too, trying to see what's going on. Great. Fun for the whole family. *Stick your noses in all together, why don't you, and catch the next show?*

"Okay, what's the problem?" Mama beats Ed to the landing. Her eyes move from one kid to the next. "I thought we were having an earthquake. You know you can't mess around on this scaffolding. Somebody could get hurt."

But Big Skinny is all smiles. "No problem, Mrs M – just a little mix-up on the bird's eyeball colour, right, guys? Miller says blue, and Mouse says gold, so I was thinking –" He stops in mid-sentence, as if something's just struck him. An actual thought – maybe his first ever, from the look on his face. His grin gets even dopier, if that's possible. "Well, that is, if it were up to *me*, I'd probably pick blue for sure. Blue's one of your most popular colours, no question about it. But *gold*, now – well, that's a whole other deal, that's all." He stops again and gives Ed this weird little nod. "You just can't beat *gold*, you know what I'm saying? I mean, if you need cheering up or anything. Everybody likes *gold*. It just has such a nice *ring* to it, right, Ed?"

He pauses for breath. Ruby stares. Good grief. Has he lost what little mind he used to have, or what?

But Ed is shaking his head as if he actually understands. "Not now, Vincent," he says quietly.

"Aw, come on, Ed –"

"This isn't the time."

"Sure it is!"

Mama looks as confused as Ruby feels. "Time for what?"

Ed's pinking up again. "Nothing, nothing at all. It's just – well, not nothing, that's not the right word, it's –

it's just the opposite, really, but this isn't how I wanted to . . . that is, we can talk about it later, when we have a little more —"

"Aw, go on, man," Mouse says suddenly. "Just give her the stupid ring. You don't want nobody stealin' it or nothin'."

For a full ten seconds, no one says a word. Ten seconds, at least. That's a long, long time. You could actually call the silence deafening, what with the roar from the main road.

Then Ed clears his throat.

Mama shakes her head. Her eyes are saying, "Not yet."

Ruby looks from one to the other.

And then she starts running.

26

She doesn't know where she's running, really. *Away*, that's all she knows, away from the eyes staring and the heads shaking and the soft hands reaching for her, trying to make her wait, the voices saying, *It's okay, Ruby, don't worry, honey, nothing's set in stone here, everything's okay.* But it's not some mountain top she ends up on, howling curses into the clear blue air. Not even the breathing place can help her, not today. It's her own room she finds herself in, her own bed she flings herself on, her own stupid words mocking her from the pile of papers on the bedside table.

Dear Mr Spielberg:
~~My name is Ruby Miller . . .~~

She picks up the pages and rips them into a thousand pieces, and throws them up into the air and lets them rain around her head like confetti at a wedding. *Strike up the band! Here she comes, the Dummy of the Year!* Stupid, stupid, stupid. What was she thinking, anyhow?

"Ruby?" Mama knocks softly.

Ruby doesn't answer.

"Ruby? Honey? Can I come in?"

No, Ruby thinks at her.

"Please, honey. We can't leave it like this."

Sure we can. How else can we leave it? Like there's really another CHOICE here? Okay, then, I choose — what? Ditch the doctor. Move back to Texas. Find Daddy and make everything right again . . .

"Ruby?"

Ruby buries her head under her pillow.

Mama comes in anyway. Pete is right behind her. Even with her ears stopped, Ruby can hear the door creak open. The footsteps getting close, the two of them standing beside the bed, breathing on her back.

She turns over finally. Sits up. Glares at both of them. What else can she do? They're not going anywhere.

They sit down, facing her, one on each side. Another endless ten seconds tick by. Then, when she can't stand it any longer:

"So when's the wedding?" Ruby asks.

"Oh, honey." Mama's voice is quiet. Reassuring. Maddeningly reasonable. "We haven't made any plans yet. There's nothing definite. I wouldn't make a decision like that without talking to you first. You know that, right?"

Ruby shrugs.

"Sure you do. Something as important as this — well, sure you do, baby."

Ruby can't quite believe what she's hearing. "Oh,

come on, Mama, are you kidding me? Like we always talk about *everything*, right? You did it just last night. You made up your own mind; you didn't ask me or Pete when you told Daddy we wouldn't meet him today. You decided that all by yourself, remember?"

Mama looks stung. She doesn't seem to have been expecting that. How could she *not* have been expecting that? "That's different," she says. "There are reasons . . . I couldn't do it again, that's all; I couldn't put you through that. Sitting there for hours, waiting and waiting, getting your hopes up that way. And for what? It's not fair to you — either of you — to anybody. I can't do it again, Ruby. You don't understand."

"*Of course* I don't understand! How could I understand? You never say anything; you never explain anything. You just cut up his pictures and move on, Mama; that's all you ever do. You don't say why, you never say why . . ."

She can't get the rest of it out. It hurts too much. The words stick in her throat in an aching furball; if she were a cat, she'd be throwing up by now.

Mama seems to be having throat trouble of her own. She climbs up beside Ruby, puts her arm around her. Opens the other one for Pete, who nestles in too. The three of them just sit there for a while, hanging on to each other. And finally Mama starts talking again, a little bit at a time:

"There are reasons, Ruby. There are reasons for everything. I've just . . . I've been trying to make it okay for you, baby, for both of you. I didn't want you to have to feel the way that . . . I just wanted us to get on with our lives . . . Was that wrong? Maybe it was wrong; I don't know . . . I know it's not fair; nothing's fair, baby. It's just life, that's all. It's not your fault, or my fault — well, maybe some of it's my fault; I'm sure some of it is . . . but I think it's more . . . it's just the way things happen sometimes. It's . . . I know I'm not making any sense here, but . . . you're just going to have to take my word for it, sweetheart. You're just going to have to trust me on this. Can't you trust me, honey?"

Pete nods anxiously. He pulls on her sleeve. "I trust you, Mama."

Mama wipes her eyes and smiles a little. She gives him another squeeze. But it's Ruby's answer she's waiting for.

"Sure I do," Ruby mumbles, when she can manage it. "You know I do. But — but it's not enough, is it? I mean, come on, Mama, isn't that just half? Seems like you could trust us, too."

Mama doesn't say anything to that. Not at first. She just sits there, breathing. Then she closes her eyes and presses on the lids with her fingertips, like she does when she has a headache. Oh, man. Ruby wishes she'd kept her mouth closed. "I'm sorry, Mama," she begins. "I didn't mean —"

"No." Mama stops her. "You're right. You deserve that much."

That's all she says for a minute. But the room feels different somehow; the *air* feels different. And slowly it dawns on Ruby: *Oh, my God. She's gonna tell us. She's really gonna tell us, isn't she? This is it, what I've been waiting for; I'm about to hear it . . .*

Suddenly she's terrified. She wants to take it back. *Never mind, Mama, YOU were right, not me. I'm not ready for this. I'm too young. Pete's too young, anyway. You've got to think of him, I can see that now. I was wrong, that's all. We've made it this far without knowing; what's another twenty or forty years?*

But she doesn't say any of that. She just sits there like the others. Breathing. Waiting.

And finally Mama starts talking again. "Frankie – your daddy – he's . . ." She shakes her head. "I don't know where to start this. I don't know how much you remember. You were both so young . . ."

"We remember," says Ruby. There's a loose orange thread hanging from one of the knots on her chenille bedspread. She gives it a tug. "Right, Pete?"

Pete nods.

"Right. Well, let's see . . ." Mama clears her throat. "He was – he's good at a lot of things. You should know that about him. At our school, he was – well, kind of a star really. Maybe not the best one on every team, but he was right up there. Football, baseball –"

"Athletics?" Pete asks.

"Athletics, too. Absolutely. All the sports."

Pete nods again, as if that explained a lot. Mama touches his cheek. Then she goes on:

"And he was funny. He could always make you laugh . . . about the craziest things." She smiles a little and waves her hand, like she's waving some old joke away. "He was everybody's best fried. Teachers, kids — everybody liked him. And girls — all the girls. He never went out with just one, until after we left school. He didn't want to hurt anybody's feelings, so he said he liked all of us."

Ruby gives the thread another tug. "But he married you."

"Right. Although — well, I couldn't believe it when he asked me. It was all so fast. And we were so young . . . I'm not sure he meant to, exactly."

Ruby's eyebrows shoot up. "How could he not *mean* to?"

Mama shakes her head again. "It's kind of hard to explain. We'd only had a couple of dates. We were both — what? Barely eighteen. And then he came to see me in that silly pageant . . . Well, you remember. I've told you about that —"

Ruby sits up straighter. "Miss Wichita Falls?"

"Right. And I was a disaster."

"No, you weren't! You were fourth runner-up!"

"My next-door neighbour was one of the judges. Believe me. I was a total disaster. I got so nervous in the interview, I said —" She covers her face with her hands. "Oh, let's just skip over that part . . ."

"What? What'd you say?"

Pete pulls her hands down. "What'd you say, Mama?"

She sighs. "When the Master of Ceremonies asked me about my life's ambition, I said I wanted to help fight crippled children."

Ruby chokes.

Pete looks shocked. "Mama!"

"I meant the *disease*, honey. Not the actual children."

"Oh."

"Still . . .!" Ruby groans. Then she bursts out laughing. "Oh, *Mama* . . ."

"I know, I know. I've been trying to forget it for fifteen years."

"And Daddy asked you to marry him after *that*?"

"I think he just felt sorry for me. I cried for about two hours straight. He was trying to cheer me up, that's all. I think he probably woke up the next day and couldn't believe what he'd gotten himself into."

Ruby stops laughing. "Did he tell you that?"

"No. Never. Not in so many words. He's not that way. It was still just like school; he wouldn't have wanted to hurt my feelings. Oh, Lord, we were both so *young* . . . It wasn't until later, when I knew him better . . . Well, I just knew, that's all. But of course by that time . . ." Her voice trails off.

"You were married?" asks Ruby.

"We were married."

Mama gets quiet again. Ruby can't let her stop *now*.

"But you were happy, weren't you?" She's thinking of *Groundhog Day* – the whole family watching, all together.

Mama nods. "We were happy. A lot of the time. The first few years, anyway. Of course there were some bad days, too. But everybody has those."

"Bad days?"

"Well, nights really. When he'd stay out till all hours and forget to call, and then come home the next morning with some wild story –"

"What kind of story?"

"Oh, you know, some billion-dollar drug bust or an armed robbery he stopped in the nick of time – that kind of thing. He wasn't even twenty-one yet, you see, when he joined the force; he wasn't finished growing up. But even then, when I'd be so furious I couldn't see straight – once I called up my cousin Sheila in Houston and said, get my room ready, I'll be there tomorrow – even *then* he'd make things okay. He'd make me laugh somehow. I never knew how he did it, but he always did. And then I couldn't stay mad. There were still mornings I'd wake up and feel just like I did the night he asked me to marry him. I couldn't believe how lucky I was – that out of all those girls, Frankie Miller had actually picked me. And then when the two of you came along . . ." Mama touches Ruby's hair, then Pete's. "I thought – we both thought – well, we've died and gone to heaven; just look at these angels."

She has to stop for a minute there, and fish a wad of Kleenex out of her pocket, and blow her nose. Pete pats her arm a little bit, and Ruby goes back to fooling with the orange thread. And then Mama takes a deep breath and keeps on talking.

"Of course there was never enough money. There never is, somehow. I got some part-time work doing child care – they didn't mind if I brought my own children along – but we still came up short. We'd write down a budget, and *try* to stick to it; I'd count the slices in a loaf of bread, practically. But it never added up at the end of the month. And I couldn't for the life of me see why. I mean, you don't get rich being on the force, but it ought to be enough to get by on. Other people did it. And your daddy was a good policeman, too; everybody said so. They all liked him down at the station. He was the first one in his class to get promoted. It was just – well, I didn't get it, that's all, why the money kept disappearing like that."

"Maybe somebody was stealing it," says Pete.

"No, honey." Mama winds up one of his red curls around her finger. "You daddy was gambling, that's all it was."

Ruby starts to get that throw-up feeling again. "You mean, like poker?"

"Not just poker. Not just card parties with the guys; it was a lot worse than that. He owed all kinds of money, to people he shouldn't have had anything to do with. More than I ever imagined. He'd win a little, and then he'd lose it all, and then he'd try to make it up, and – well, it just goes on and on like that. You never come out ahead in the long run; you just keep getting in deeper than before."

"He told you that?" Ruby asks.

Mama sighs. "No, baby. He never told me. He has a hard time admitting things like that. He has a thousand explanations – I think he half-believes them himself. They say the best liars always believe their own lies."

Ruby gives the orange thread a jerk, snapping it off finally, leaving a ragged half-inch gap in the chenille. "Maybe they weren't lies," she says. "Maybe he was telling you the truth."

Mama shakes her head. "That's what I wanted to think. What I did think. For years, Ruby. But it got harder and harder. The lying was just . . . in the air we breathed, somehow. It's hard to explain now. There were . . . whispers, weird phone calls in the middle of the night, charges on our credit card he said were mistakes. And our credit — it was a mess by this time. You'd both been sick off and on that whole winter; there were extra medical bills, things our health insurance didn't cover. Frankie said not to worry about it; he was getting a raise soon. It would all be fine. But none of it was true. Nothing was fine. And then . . . oh, boy . . ." Mama stops again. She's trembling, just a little; she has to hold on tight to Ruby and Pete until it passes. "Are you sure you want to hear all of this? I'm afraid it doesn't get any easier."

Ruby looks at Pete. He nods. He seems okay. A little paler than usual maybe. It makes his freckles stand out, as if they're in 3-D. As for Ruby — she doesn't know how she feels any more. Unless this is how it is when they put you in hyper-sleep for the journey to Mars. It's beyond sick now — more like mummification. She can't move; she can't do anything but sit there. She doesn't really want to hear the rest, but she has to, that's all. She has to. She grits her teeth. "Keep going."

Mama takes another deep breath. "They said . . . witnesses said . . ." She stops. Tries again. "Do you know what a bribe is?"

Ruby just sits there. Pete nods. "Bribe wire. Like I got stuck on that time at Cub Scout camp."

"No, baby. That's barbed wire. This is — well, it's money someone takes from another person, like — well, like a criminal. Someone who's done something wrong. And say you're a policeman, and you know about this guy's crime — illegal gambling or — or whatever it is. And you ought to arrest him for it. You know that's what you're supposed to do. But maybe you're in trouble, like your daddy was. Maybe you feel desperate or — well, you're just not thinking straight. And this person — this criminal — he says, 'Look, I've got all this cash, more than I need. How about I give you some, help you out a little — just until you get on your feet again? And all you have to do is forget about me; forget you ever saw me. What can it hurt?' And maybe this policeman — he's feeling so trapped now, he makes the wrong decision. He says okay. He takes the guy's offer. That's what a bribe is."

"Oh." Pete nods again. "Hush money."

Mama's eyes get wide. "Hush money?" She looks at Ruby, but Ruby is still mummified.

"Like in *The Sting*," says Pete.

"Oh. Right."

"It was on the Film Classics Channel last week."

"Right. Well. Anyway. That's pretty much what happened, I guess. With your daddy. He owed all this money to the wrong people, and then he tried to get out of it by accepting this — this other money. And the department found out. There were undercover officers who knew all about it, a whole investigation. And then a trial, and —"

Ruby covers her ears. *Don't say it, it can't be true, none of it's true, I'm dreaming, I'm not hearing any of this . . .*

Ever so gently, Mama takes down her hands, holds them in her own.

Pete pulls on her sleeve. "Our daddy went to *jail?*"

Mama nods. "For three years." She's still holding tight to Ruby. "I'm sorry, honey. I'm so sorry."

27

FADE IN:

DEEP SPACE. DESTINATION: UNKNOWN.
Sealed tight in her hyper-baric rocket capsule, THE
GIRL sleeps on.

                    FIRST ALIEN (VOICE-OVER)
          We're getting a visual on the humanoid now,
          Commander. Vital signs holding steady.
          Minimal heart rate; no appreciable motor
          activity; temporary paralysis of synaptic
          systems due to an overload of incoming
          information in the thermonuclear control
          centre, reducing brain waves to an all but
          indiscernible blip . . .

          "Ruby?"

          . . . on the hexathrombic screen.

SECOND ALIEN
Excellent work, Lieutenant. We're proceeding
on schedule then?

FIRST ALIEN
Exactly as planned, sir. We have secretly
boarded the craft through a series of mind-
links with unsuspecting crew members and
are attempting at this moment to infiltrate the
girl's subconscious, implanting disinformation
as directed. Naturally she struggles to resist
us . . .

"I know it's not easy, honey . . ."

FIRST ALIEN
But we need not worry. She is powerless
against our superior intelligence, unable to
shut out our whispers, transfixed by the sound
of our oddly familiar voices murmuring
soothingly in her –

"Ruby. Please. Talk to me, baby. Are you okay?"
She manages to nod finally. Nothing's changed. Not
on the outside, anyway. She's not in a spaceship; she's
still sitting with Mama and Pete on her bed, in her room,
in their apartment on Valleyheart Drive, in the middle of
a hot afternoon on the third Saturday in August.

But on the *inside*, where it matters, she's fifty trillion
light-years past Pluto.

Mama is still studying her face. "Is there anything else you'd like to ask me? Either of you? Anything you don't understand?"

Anything? If Ruby only knew where to start; if her voice were working . . . But she doesn't. It isn't. So she just sits there. *Silent as a stone, a tombstone maybe, like somebody just died.*

SECOND ALIEN
You don't think she suspects, do you?

FIRST ALIEN
Highly doubtful. But possible.

SECOND ALIEN
Better double the putridium paralaxium, just
to be on the safe side.

"Well," says Mama. She touches Ruby's cheek once more. "I know it's a lot to take in all at once. Maybe we should leave it there for now. It's after one o'clock; you must be starving. I'll mix up a little tuna, how's that?"

Ruby shakes her head.

"Oh, come on, honey; you'll feel better if you eat something. Aren't you hungry at all? Pete's hungry, right, Pete?"

"Kind of," says Pete. He sounds like he's apologising.

But Mama looks relieved. "All right then. So I guess I'll just — now wait, we're out of tuna, aren't we? How about . . . I'll run over the McDonald's and pick us up some hamburgers. Special treat. Extra onions and pickles, right, Ruby? And on Pete's — don't tell me — hold the mayo, ketchup, onions, lettuce, tomatoes —"

"And gherkin," says Pete.

"Right. No gherkin." Mama starts towards the door. "And then maybe after lunch, we could go to a film. Would you like that? They can get by without us at the wall this once."

She might as well be speaking Neptunian, for all the reaction that gets. *Are there films on Mars?* Ruby wonders dully.

Mama gives her a long look. "You sure you're okay?"

Ruby nods again, even though okay isn't really the word for the way she's feeling right now. But it's not exactly a lie either; she can't tell how she is. She's not the one in charge any more. You'd have to ask *Them*.

FIRST ALIEN

Subject still firmly in hand, Commander. Response to mention of food negative in the extreme. Provokes change in coloration: note green around gills.

SECOND ALIEN

Splendid progress. Transmutation is under way, then?

FIRST ALIEN

No question about it. At this rate, she'll be one of us by sundown.

"I'll be right back," says Mama.

And then she's gone, and the front door is opening and closing, leaving Ruby and Pete staring at each other.

Another minute crawls by. Miss Pierce's phone starts ringing in the other half of the block. They can hear it clearly through the wall, ringing on and on. Why doesn't she answer? Ruby wonders thickly through the blue haze in her brain. Unless it's just Lord Byron again. He does kettles and car alarms, too. Once Mama almost called the cops, but it was only the bird.

The ringing stops, finally.

"Maybe they got it wrong," says Pete.

Ruby doesn't understand. The haze is too dense. His lips are moving, but he's not making any sense. *Who got what wrong? The person on the phone?* She doesn't say it; she just thinks it at him. But he seems to hear her anyway.

"The judge and them," says Pete. "Maybe they got the wrong guy."

Ruby sits up a little straighter.

"You know, like that time *you* got arrested."

A tingle runs along Ruby's backbone. Just the tiniest sensation at first: infinitesimal pinpricks of light . . . heat . . . something. *Wait a minute . . . Wait a minute . . .*

"Maybe there were some of those extenutive — extenutory —"

"Extenuating circumstances?"

"Yeah. Some of those."

FIRST ALIEN

Red alert! Red alert! Who let that kid in the capsule? He's tampering with the hyper-sleep apparatus!

SECOND ALIEN

Well, fix it, you imbecile! Get rid of him!

FIRST ALIEN

I'm trying, sir . . .

"Say that again," says Ruby. Her voice is working. How about that?

"Maybe they got it wrong. Maybe he was hypnotised, like on *Hawaii Five-0*. Or maybe he had amnesia. That was one of the best episodes. You know, when the bad guy hit Danno in the head and planted the money on him, and when Danno came to, he couldn't remember what happened?"

Ruby shakes herself a little, like you do when your foot's gone to sleep, and you have to wake it up, even though it prickles like fire and frostbite together. She doesn't want to hurt Pete's feelings or anything, but those old television shows are pretty far-fetched. Somebody's *always* getting hypnotised or losing their memory or turning out to have an evil twin. She sighs. For a minute there, it almost made sense. "I don't know, Pete. You heard Mama. She said there were witnesses."

"Oh sure, they always have them." Pete shrugs. "They

could have got hypnotised too. Or maybe *they* were the bad guys."

"Who? The witnesses?"

"Well, sure. How do you know *they* were telling the truth?"

"Because . . . because they wouldn't just . . ." Ruby's spine starts tingling again. *Wait a minute . . .* How *does* she know? "You mean like . . . like in *The Fugutive*? When everybody thought Harrison Ford was the murderer?"

"Right," says Pete. "Just like that."

"But it was really the one-armed man who did it! And Harrison kept telling everybody and telling everybody, but nobody believed him . . ."

"They all thought he was lying . . ."

"So they sent him to jail."

"But then that bus crashed into the train . . ."

"And he escaped . . ."

"But that FBI guy wouldn't stop chasing him . . ."

"Right! So Daddy – I mean Harrison – he had to go into hiding, remember? He had to find the one-armed man himself to prove he was innocent!"

Pete shook his head. "Yeah, but . . ."

"But what?"

"Well, our daddy didn't have to escape, did he? He got out of jail just regular."

"So?"

"So why didn't he come to dinner all those times?"

"Because . . . because . . . well, maybe he was just – just *lost*, or . . ."

FIRST ALIEN
She's wavering, Commander. Perhaps we spoke
too soon. It appears the brother is with us after
all . . .

Ruby makes a mighty effort. "Or *something,* I don't
know. It might be anything. We need to *ask* him, that's
all! Maybe he'd have come this time if Mama hadn't said
no. We don't know for sure, right? Not until we ask. If
we could just *talk* to him ourselves once, maybe he could
explain. And then if it turns out he's still trying to find
the real perpetrator or whatever — well, we could *help*
him. Right?"
Pete thinks that over.
"Well, couldn't we?"
He nods. "I guess so."

SECOND ALIEN
Well, are you just going to STAND there,
Lieutenant? What are you waiting for? Send in
the reinforcements.

FIRST ALIEN
I'm doing the best I can, sir. I can't understand
it; the system seems to be approaching total
meltdown . . .

Ruby is on her feet now, pacing. She's alive again;
she's back; she's shooting sparks. "We've got to find
him, that's all. There has to be a way to find him.

Maybe we could hire a private investigator or something."

"Doesn't that cost a lot of money?"

"Well, yeah, probably. But I might be able to get some together pretty soon." Ruby looks at the scraps of her letter and screenplay, scattered all over the place. *Rats*. What'd she have to do that for? Well, that's okay; she'll just have to remember what she wrote, that's all. It shouldn't be that hard; it only took her a couple of days the first time. How long does it take to get an advance on these things, anyway? She'll probably have to have an agent handle all the details. There was a whole list of 'em in one of those library books, wasn't there? Maybe she ought to run over there right now and . . .

"I don't know, Ruby. Seems like it's be a lot cheaper if we just found him ourselves."

"Oh, come on, Pete. How are we gonna do that? We don't even know where he lives, remember? You think Mama's gonna tell us? After everything she said? How're we supposed to find him? There are ten million people in this town."

The front door opens and closes. "Lunch is here!" Mama calls.

"His name's in the phone book," says Pete.

28

FLASH FORWARD: Monday morning.

Thunder rumbles, though the sky is blue.

Ruby opens her eyes. *This is the day I'll find him.*

She lies very still for a minute, listening to the sounds she always hears in the morning: Mama turning on the tap in the kitchen, the kettle whistling, plumbing rattling, pipes making their usual loud burping noise when someone (Pete's up already then?) turns off the shower. And under all this, that low-down rumble grumbling from outside somewhere.

Thunder? Come on. In August? No way.

Not that it wouldn't be welcome in this heat. They could use a good rainstorm right about now. The weather's been weird for three straight days. Not just regular hot — you expect that this time of year — but sticky, muggy, hazy hot. Something peculiar in the air — some kind of yellow-brown yuck, hiding the mountains, hanging heavy over the whole Valley.

But it couldn't be thunder, could it? Not today.

Ruby looks out of her window and sees Miss Pierce with the bird on her head, rolling the big black rubbish bin out to the kerb. *Rumble, rumble, rumble . . .*

Well, of course. Thank God. Ruby takes a deep breath, lets it out slowly. They don't have time to be fooling around with rain, today of all days.

Speaking of time . . . She reaches for her glasses, checks the clock on the bedside table. Nearly eight already? Good Lord. She jumps out of bed, starts rushing around. She didn't mean to sleep so late; she's got to be ready to go just as soon as Mama leaves for work. They couldn't do anything about finding Daddy all weekend, with her right there looking at them, worrying over how they were taking this whole thing. And now time is running out. For real. That's not only Ruby's imagination either; it was on TV just last night. She was up till eleven-thirty listening to some scientist explain it: how little by little, the moon is moving away from the earth, so its gravity is pulling less and less. Which causes the earth to spin faster and travel faster around the sun. So that now, according to this guy — here's the part that really got Ruby — every year is one five hundred thousandth of a second shorter than the one before.

Okay, sure, it's not *that* much. It just makes her feel pressed, that's all. Clearly, there's not a millisecond to waste.

"Good morning!" Mama's just finishing her tea when Ruby joins her and Pete at the breakfast table. "Sleep well?"

"Fine," says Ruby, sliding into her chair. It's weird; she has this sudden stab of guilt. She feels like she's lying, even though she isn't; it's perfectly true – she slept okay. It's just . . . well, she's left out some things the last couple of days. But she can't help it, can she? If they told Mama everything – like where they're planning to go in the next half-hour – she'd only say no, it was a bad idea. And then Ruby would just feel weirder. Because she has to go. She just has to, now that she knows where to look.

"He's in the *phone book*?" was all she could say when Pete told her. She had never felt so stupid in her entire life. How come *she* never thought of looking in the phone book? Not once in all this time? Of course she'd always thought of their daddy as living in Texas, that was part of it. Even after the calls started, she'd just figured he was in town on a case or something. Still, somewhere in there, you'd think it might have at least *crossed her mind*. Turns out it was no trouble at all for a seven-year-old.

"But why didn't you ever say anything?" Ruby whispered. (Mama was just in the next room.)

"You never asked me," Pete whispered back.

Oh. Well. Lucky there was at least *one* genius in the family. Because there it was, in black and white, when Ruby had a chance to check, right in between a dozen F. Millers and half a dozen actual Franks:

Miller, Francis P. 3502½ Mountain Laurel Ln . . .

She could hardly believe her eyes. That was him, no question about it. Francis P.; P. for Peter, just like Pete. He was always proud of being named for Daddy. All of which was amazing enough by itself. But then Ruby took *another* look in the book, just to make sure she wasn't seeing things, and that was when she just about fainted –

"Wait a minute! Mountain Laurel Lane? Are you kidding me? That's the Enchanted Highway!"

Pete stared at her. "The what?"

"In the PRP –"

"The what?"

"The Planet of Rich People!"

But Pete looked at her like she'd lost her mind, so she gave up trying to translate. "I'll just have to show you when we go," she said finally. Even though the whole rest of the weekend, it felt as if her head were about to explode. Their dad lived on the Enchanted Highway!

What are the odds on a thing like that? she wonders now, sprinkling sugar on her Rice Krispies.

It has to be another sign, right? What else *could* it be? How many times has she passed his house and never had any idea? It's as if someone is sending her secret messages all in code, or buried treasure maps, where everything has two meanings. Or one of those crazy Magic Eye pictures from the calendar right above Pete's head – just a bunch of random dots when you first look at it. But if you keep looking and keep looking and let your eyes slip out of focus just a little – the way you do when you're half-awake and just about to drift off into a

214

dream – all of a sudden there it *is*, so clear it takes your breath away: horses galloping down a race track, or a lady watering her garden, or Santa and his eight tiny reindeer flying past the moon . . .

And then of course your eyes get tired, and you blink, and the picture vanishes, and you're back to a bunch of disconnected dots that don't mean a thing. But once you've seen it – even for a moment – well, then you know it's there, that's the difference. That it's been there all along, just waiting for you to notice.

Which house is it? The pink one? The grey one? They're all so beautiful. He must be doing okay then. He must have found a new job and saved up so he could get a place with plenty of room. It all makes sense, if you think about it – after what he's been through – being falsely accused and everything. He's probably planning to surprise us once he gets his name cleared, so then the whole family can move in together, and . . .

"You don't have any special plans today, do you?" asks Mama.

Ruby takes a deep breath. No getting around this one. There's no work scheduled at the wall today, so she can't use that as a cover. It's supposed to dry for the next forty-eight hours before they can start the last coat. "No, ma'am," she says with her face on fire. "Nothing much."

Mama's eyes linger on her just a fraction of a second longer than usual. But then she nods. "Well then, if you have a chance, would you mind dropping off the library books? I've left them in a stack by the door. They're due today."

"Oh. Sure." Ruby exhales.

"And then maybe your two could pick up something for yourselves – you're all done with those summer reading lists, right? Something just for fun. Or maybe even catch that film now; they're rerunning *E.T.* over at the cinema. I think we can still afford it this week." She starts rooting around in her purse, comes out with an only slightly wrinkled ten-dollar bill and two dollars in change. "Might as well have one last fling before school starts, right?"

"Right," says Ruby. There's that stabbing again. "Thanks." She puts the money in her jeans pocket, being careful not to look at Pete, who is certain to be looking at least as guilty as she feels.

Mama snaps her purse closed. Starts to stand up. Then she sits down again and takes Ruby's hand. "Honey . . ."

Ruby's heart skips a beat. *She knows, doesn't she? She always knows. She must've heard us talking, or –*

"I just want to tell you – both of you – how proud I am of the way that . . . well, the way that you've been dealing with – with all this hard news and everything."

Ruby doesn't know what to say to that, so she just sits there.

"The thing is . . ." Mama clears her throat. "The thing is, you were right. All these years – I should have trusted you, that's all. I guess . . . well, I guess sometimes I just forget you're not babies any more."

Oh, God. Why should *that* make Ruby feel like such a jerk? But fortunately just then Pete knocks over his orange juice, and Mama is too busy running for a dishcloth and getting everything all mopped up to notice Ruby's peculiar shade of purple. And by the time that crisis is over, she's late for work; she's grabbing her bag again and giving them both a quick kiss and hurrying out of the door.

Oh, man. Ruby and Pete stare at each other as the Demon coughs and splutters and catches, finally, then lurches off down the street.

"Don't look at me like that," says Ruby. "We've got to find him, don't we?"

Pete scratches his elbow. "Maybe we ought to tell her first."

"Oh, come on, Pete . . ." Ruby takes hold of his shoulders. She needs help; she's floundering here; she feels split right down the middle, as if Mama and Daddy are grabbing an ear apiece and pulling as hard as they can in opposite directions. "She'll be glad, once she understands. Once we know the whole story. Everything will be better then. Right?"

Still no answer. The earth is spinning like a top now. No telling how many five hundred thousandths of a second are gone for ever . . .

"Right, Pete?"

Pete nods. "Right."

29

9.37 a.m., 34°, reads the big time/temperature sign on the Mid-Valley Bank building.

"How much further?" asks Pete.

"Not too much," says Ruby. "Just a couple of miles."

"I have to go to the loo."

"Didn't you go before we left?"

Pete sighs. "I drank two glasses of orange juice."

Good grief. It never occurred to Ruby to include toilet stops on their hike to the Enchanted Highway. If they have to walk home and start all over again, it'll be noon before they get there. "Well, how bad is it? Can you make it to Daddy's place?"

Pete thinks it over. "I guess so."

"If you're desperate, we can try to find one around here somewhere."

Pete looks to his right, then his left: two banks, one Blockbuster, three furniture stores, one bridal boutique . . . "I'm not that desperate."

Ruby pats his shoulder. "Just a couple of miles, that's all."

Man, it's hot. By the time they cross Ventura, they're both dripping with sweat. It's been a while since Ruby was south of the boulevard; they've been so busy with the wall and everything. Plus this really isn't walking weather. Even most of her acquaintances in the Domain of Dogs are nowhere to be seen today. But then this is the PRP; they're probably just taking it east in their air-conditioned dog houses.

All except for the fat black Lab, that is, who comes bounding out joyfully from her post at the little blue cottage on the corner, the second the Miller kids' feet hit the pavement on Mountain Laurel Lane.

"Hey, Thelma! How you been, girl?" asks Ruby, scratching her behind the ears. "This is my brother, Pete. Say hello to Pete . . . Oh, come on, don't lick him to death."

"It's okay," says Pete, grinning, as Thelma slobbers his whole face with dog kisses. "I don't mind."

"GOOD MORNING, SUNSHINE!" roars a voice. "HOW ARE YOU TODAY?"

Ruby and Pete look up and see Thelma's master waving at them. Ruby didn't really expect him to be out already — it's too early for a ball game — but the old man is there in his regular deck-chair under the twin palms, just like always. He's got the newspaper spread out on the grass all around him and a straw hat on his head, and his transistor radio is blaring out a tune on the oldies station: "Stop! In the name of love . . ."

"FINE, THANKS!" Ruby yells back, and then she gives Thelma one last pat and starts up the hill.

"Wait a minute!" calls Pete. "Look! Thirty-five-oh-two!"

"Where?" Ruby hasn't seen any street numbers yet. She's just been assuming Daddy's house would be one of the big places up higher. (She's sort of halfway settled on the brown mansion with the stained-glass windows.)

"Right there!" Pete points at a set of cracked address tiles on the old man's cottage, half hidden under the yellow roses twining around the door.

Ruby squints behind her lenses. Good thing Pete's eyes are better than hers. There it is all right: 3502. Are they already that close? She looks all around. Would 3502½ be next door then? No, the number there is 3504 . . . And the one across the street is 3503. so where's —

"CAN I HELP YOU?" the old man roars, waving them over.

Pete tugs on Ruby's elbow, worrying. "We're not supposed to talk to strangers," he whispers.

"He's not a stranger," says Ruby. "He's the Gatekeeper." But she takes Pete's hand anyway, just to be on the safe side.

For once, he doesn't snatch it away. "The Gate-keeper?"

"It's okay," she says, and with Thelma rushing ecstatically before them — *Oh goody, oh gosh, can you believe it? They've come to PLAY!* — they start up the flower-lined cobblestones that lead to the deck-chair.

"Kind of a hot day for a walk," says the old man, smiling and flipping off the music. He can talk in a normal tone of voice then. That's a relief.

"Yes, sir," says Ruby. "Oh no, please. You don't have to get up —"

But he's already rising — slowly and painfully — creaking all the way to his feet. (*See there, Pete, that's a real gentleman*, Mama would say if she were here.) "Oh, that's all right. Nearly time for my trampoline lesson, anyhow." He gives Pete a wink, then lifts his straw hat. "David R. Davis, at your service. And of course you know Thelma." He nods towards the dog, who is so beside herself with delight over the unexpected turn the morning seems to be taking that she suddenly collapses, just keels right over in a furry black heap amongst the marigolds.

"Is she okay?" asks Pete.

The old man chuckles. "She's fine." He leans over and rubs her belly. "You'll have to excuse her. She faints when she gets overly excited. The last time we had company was just before World War Two."

Ruby smiles and shakes hands. "I'm Ruby. And this is Pete."

"A pleasure," says Mr Davis. "You're not lost, are you?"

"Not exactly," says Ruby. "This is Mountain Laurel Lane, right? We're looking for thirty-five-oh-two and a half, but we can't find the half."

"Why, you've found it," says Mr Davis. "It's just around the back, over the garage."

"Oh." It takes a couple of second for that to sink in. A garage flat? Okay. So she was wrong; so it's not a big house. So what? Who cares? Just as long as Daddy's in it. "Well, all right then. Thanks." She half-turns to go, then remembers her manners and turns back. "Is it okay if we go back there?"

Mr Davis strokes the short white crop of stubble on his chin. "Well, you're certainly welcome to wait, but there's no one there right now. Were you looking for Frank Miller?"

"Yes, sir," says Ruby as best she can over the sudden pounding of her heart. Just hearing his name said out loud like that makes her weak at the knees. It's all she can do to keep from falling over like Thelma. This is it then, isn't it? They've come to the right place. They're welcome to wait – *welcome to wait* – after so much waiting . . .

"Is he expecting you?" Mr Davis asks.

Pete gives Ruby a look: *I told you so; I told you we should have called.* He'd wanted to all along, but Ruby said no. If they called – well, you never know with grown-ups. Daddy might even side with Mama – anything is possible – he might tell them not to come. Ruby couldn't take a chance like that. And besides, she wanted to surprise him; she wanted to see his face when he saw them standing there in front of him. She'd imagined it so many times – how it would light up – how at first he wouldn't be able to believe it, and then he'd see it was true, it was really them. And then he'd open his arms, and after that, whatever came next would be all right.

Of course, she knew he might not be there. He might be at work, she realised that. That was okay; she had a plan there too. She'd written him a letter. It's right here in her pocket, next to the blue yo-yo. Just a short letter – only a note, really – but it said everything he needed to know. Once he read that, he would come to *them*; she was sure of it. But for now –

"No, sir," she says. "He's not expecting us. But – well, we just wanted to see him. We're his kids."

Mr Davis plainly wasn't ready for that one. His amazingly bushy eyebrows shoot up. "Is that right?" he says. "Well, how about that? Frank never mentioned any . . . that is . . . well, isn't that wonderful? Your dad's a fine fellow. A mighty fine fellow. You wouldn't believe the mess this place was in before he started working here. We couldn't get along without him, could we, Thelma?"

Thelma thumps her tail, twitches a little. It looks like she's coming around.

"He works for you?"

"Yes, ma'am, I'm glad to say he does. Just a little more than a year now. It was Thelma here arranged the whole thing."

"Thelma?"

Thump, thump . . .

Mr Davis chuckles. "Well, Frank just happened to walk by, you see, and she ran out, and he spoke to her, same as you always do. Matter of fact, I bet it wasn't more than five minutes after you'd passed that day. So she was already keyed up, that was part of it. And then Frank got to playing with her, and the silly old thing had one of her fainting spells, just like you saw there.

And of course he was afraid she was dead – thought he'd killed her somehow. So then we got to talking . . . Well, it was just one of those lucky accidents, I guess, him looking for work right when I was looking for somebody to help out around here."

"Wow," says Ruby. The magic dots are dancing again.

"Yes, ma'am, lucky for me. These old legs have kind of given out on me, you see; they're not good for much – well, aside from the trampoline, of course." He gives Pete another wink. "And Thelma couldn't understand why nobody was walking her, and the house had to have a paint job – the neighbours had actually started complaining, can you believe it? So until Frank came along, I was pretty much up a – well, look here," he says, as an old black pick-up truck comes around the corner. "Here he is now. HEY, FRANK!" he shouts and waves. "LOOK WHO'S HERE!"

Pete's hand, which has been nothing but a soggy lump in Ruby's ever since they stepped into the yard, suddenly clamps on to her like a vice. "I have to go to the toilet," he whispers.

But Ruby can't move. *Oh, God.* "Just a minute, Pete. Please, just one more minute . . ."

The pick-up pulls into the driveway. Then sits there with its engine idling. It's stopped a little way back from them, facing them, with the sun shining on the windscreen. So you can't really see inside, even though the side windows must be down; Ruby can hear country music playing on the radio. The tune sounds familiar, but she can't quite make out the words . . .

"LOOK WHO'S HERE, FRANK!" Mr Davis shouts again.

The engine shuts off, finally. The music quits playing. The truck door opens.

And Frankie Miller gets out.

"Hey, Daddy," says Ruby. Pete's hand clamps even tighter. "It's us."

30

She thought he'd be taller.

But then that was dumb; she was just *shorter* the last time she saw him, right? She was only seven then, same as Pete is now. She must look as changed to him as he does to her.

He's grown a beard, that's a big part of it. Not a real long one or anything; it just makes his face seem different, that's all. At least, what you can see of his face. There's a beat-up baseball cap on his head, so it's hard to tell much about him, really. He could be bald under there for all Ruby knows; she couldn't even swear his eyes are still blue. The truth is, that guy Big Skinny tackled on the jogging path looked more like her dad than her dad does.

Not that any of that matters now. They've found him, that's all that counts. This is where he's supposed to open his arms, and Ruby and Pete run to him, and the music swells, and the credits start rolling . . .

But he must not have gotten the script; he's still just standing there.

Maybe they made a mistake. Maybe there's another Francis P. Miller. Maybe –

"Does your mother know you're here?" he asks.

Thelma recognises him, anyway. At the sound of his voice, she lifts her head, struggles to her feet and stretches, then goes bounding to his side. He puts out a hand – absently, as if he hardly knows he's doing it – and scratches her behind the ears. But his eyes never leave Ruby and Pete.

"No, sir," says Ruby. "Not exactly."

This doesn't appear to surprise him much. Neither does it appear to be the answer he was hoping for. "She'll be worrying," he says. "We ought to call her." He turns back towards the door, starts unloading bags. "Just let me get these groceries put away, and –"

"NO!" says Mr Davis, so loudly and unexpectedly that Ruby and Pete both jump. (They'd forgotten he was still right there behind them.) "I'll take those; you visit with your children."

"Thanks," says Frankie, "but they're kind of heavy; just let me –"

"NO, NO! Do me good; get the blood circulating." The old man limps over and lifts the bags out of Frankie's hands. "I guess we can still manage a couple of measly little grocery bags, can't we, Thelma? Come on now, you come with me. I believe there are some fine dog biscuits in here that might be of interest to you . . ." And then he tells Ruby and Pete it was a pleasure meeting them and asks if he can bring them a cold drink or anything, but they shake their heads no thanks, so he says, "Well, maybe next time," and "Come on, Thelma . . . I said, COME ON, THELMA!" And then he limps off into the house, and eventually — tail drooping, ears sagging, even her fur looking reluctant — the dog lumbers after him.

"We really ought to call your mother," says Frankie.

"No, please; not — not yet," Ruby stammers. "She's at work; she's not worried. I'm in charge till she gets home. We just wanted . . . we wanted . . ." Well, shoot, what *did* they want? Suddenly she can hardly remember. "We just wanted to . . . to tell you . . ." *Oh, for crying out loud, just SAY it, girl!* But she can't think *how* to say it; she can't think of the words. What's wrong with her anyway? She's pictured this scene a million times in the past five years, thought of a million perfect words, and now she can't think of one. Not even one. *Please, dear God, please help me think of something . . .*

And then she remembers the note — the one she was planning to leave for him if he was out. It's all in there, right? Everything he really needs to know? She unlatches Pete's hand from hers, reaches in her back pocket for the envelope, hands it to her father.

He turns it over. FRANK P. MILLER is printed neatly on the front. He looks at that for a moment. Then he looks back at Ruby. "You want me to read it now?"

She nods.

He looks at Pete. Pete nods too.

Frankie hesitates a moment. Then he opens the envelope. Ruby watches while he takes out the piece of paper inside, watches while he unfolds it, bit by bit (she folded it about ten times, for privacy). Then waits for him to read the words she knows are written there:

> *Dear Daddy,*
> *We believe you.*
> *Your children,*
> *Ruby and Pete Miller*

He just stands there for a little while, studying the paper. *Now*, thinks Ruby. *Now he knows he can trust us. Now everything will be all right* . . . And then he starts refolding, taking his time about it, being careful to get the creases exactly as they were before.

Ruby waits. She can scarcely breathe.

He clears his throat. "Your mother — she told you what happened?"

"Yes, sir," says Ruby.

He nods. "I see. Well, then . . ." He clears his throat again. He must have something caught in there. "Well, then, you already know everything you need to —"

"We know you didn't do it," Ruby blurts out.

"Like in *The Fugitive*," says Pete.

Frankie looks confused. "*The Fugitive*?"

"The film," says Ruby.

"Oh. Sure." Frankie takes off his baseball cap, runs his fingers through his hair, as it it's paining him some way. (But at least he still *has* hair, Ruby is relieved to see — curly brown, just like she remembers). Then he puts the cap back on. "Harrison Ford, right?"

"Right," says Ruby. "And he kept trying to explain; he told everybody he wasn't guilty, but no one believed him, not even the judge. Maybe not even some of his own family."

Frankie nods. "Right. I remember that one." He's quiet for a moment, thinking that over.

"So that's how we knew," says Pete.

"I see." Frankie looks down at the note. He's got it folded perfectly now. He puts it back in the envelope, holds it out to Ruby. "Thank you for this," he says. "But you've got the wrong guy."

"No!" Ruby pushes it away. What's he talking about? "No, we don't; you're in the phone book."

"I'm not who you think I am. I'm not Harrison Ford. I'm sorry . . ." He shakes his head. "You'll never know how sorry. But it's your mother you should believe."

Nobody says anything for a second or two. A hot little breeze – as hot as if it came straight from a blast furnace – springs up out of nowhere, whispering through the grass, stirring the rose petals. The palm trees dip and sway high above Ruby's head, with a rushing, swishing sound, like a far-off crowd roaring maybe, or waves crashing on sand.

"I really have to go to the toilet," says Pete.

"Oh. Sure. Of course." Frankie looks more than ready to have the subject changed. He points behind Ruby to the garage flat. The driveway curves, so you can just see the edge of it from here. "My place is right back there, up the stairs. It's not locked or anything. Want me to take you?"

"That's okay," says Pete. "I can find it." *I'm seven years old*, is what he means.

"Right," says Frankie. He watches Pete walk away. "He got so big," he says — almost as if he's just talking to himself — as if Ruby weren't here at all. "You both got so big."

What do YOU care?

Somebody — something — mutters the words in Ruby's head. She doesn't say them aloud. She doesn't even know where they came from. They frighten her a little — the coldness of them. They sound ugly. Bitter. Ugly *and* bitter. But there's something satisfying about them, too — even just the idea of them — like the thought of ripping off a scab or giving a good swift kick to someone who really deserves it. *And ye shall know the truth, and the truth shall make you free* . . . Who said that, anyway? What a crock. Free of what? Of who? And *how*, exactly? All she asked him was to tell her he didn't do it. She'd have done anything, gone anywhere, fought anybody who needed fighting. She'd have died for him if that's what it took; dying would be a snap compared to this. It was easier when she didn't know anything; it was easier when she thought *he* was dead. He always lied, Mama said; why not *now*, when it mattered? When it might have done some good? All those years, all that time she wasted believing in him . . . she thought she understood before; she thought her Magic Eye was working, but it wasn't. She didn't understand any-thing. But now she's blinked, that's what she's done, only instead of a bunch of disconnected dots, she sees the *real* picture – the picture behind the picture. In that one blink, five years just disappeared, and what might be ancient history for some people is *now* for Ruby – it's all happening *now*, this very moment – cut-up snapshots on the old blue rug and mouldy mermaids in that crummy motel and Mama crying and crying . . . *He* did that, didn't he? *He* made Mama cry – this impostor – this stranger with the beard – not her own daddy, not her laughing policeman daddy who *locked up* guys like this.

"Why didn't you come?" she asks him. "All those times. At the restaurants. Why didn't you ever come?"

"I was there," he says. "I was always there. Across the street – across the room once. All I had to do was walk a few more steps. But I couldn't . . ."

"Why not?" She says it without pity. There's no pity in her. Her heart feels rock-hard, like that lump of petrified wood Miss Pierce gave Pete for his birthday.

Frankie shakes his head. "I don't know. You all just looked . . . so good. I couldn't . . . interrupt. I was afraid I'd mess it up again."

Ruby stares at him. For a second she's almost detached – coldly curious – as if she's a robot scientist and he's a specimen on a Petri dish. She sees all, knows all, feels nothing. "You were afraid?" she repeats. It's not a question, really; it's an accusation.

He looks up from under the cap. His eyes are still blue after all. "Afraid," he says quietly.

Pete's back from the bathroom.

"Come on," Ruby mutters, grabbing his hand. "It's time to go."

"But we just got here," says Pete.

"Come *on*, Pete." She grits her teeth. "You heard what he said. We were wrong, okay? That's not him."

"Yes, it is. What are you talking about?" Pete looks at – at whoever he is. "Tell her. Tell her who you are."

He shakes his head. "There's nothing else to tell."

"But –"

"Your sister's right. Y'all should go home. I have work to do."

Pete doesn't budge. "I could help you."

"No, thanks. I can manage."

"I know how to paint stuff."

Ruby tugs on his arm. "Come *on*, Pete . . ."

There's that rushing sound again, high above them. The palm trees bend and shudder.

"Looks like rain," says the stranger, studying the sky. It's filling up with clouds. They give off a peculiar light, some sickly shade of green Ruby never saw before. He turns back to the children. "Y'all better get in the truck. I'll drive you over there. You can't walk all that way in this heat, anyhow."

"Yes, we can," says Ruby.

"No, you can't." His voice is gruff. "Go on now. Didn't you hear me? Get in the truck."

Pete breaks away from Ruby, climbs on in the cab.

But she just stands there, glaring.

The stranger takes off his cap, just like before, runs his fingers through his hair, puts it back on. Breathes in and out, a couple of deep breaths. And then he says it once more. A little softer, this time. "Come on, Ruby. Just get in the truck, okay? I need to take you home."

31

CUT TO:

The far-off purple mountains; where a lone condor is circling, high above his nest. There's an odd new wind blowing in from the sea, but the condor won't waste his strength fighting it. He settles in his rocky home, blinks his great golden eyes, draws in his enormous wings.

The wind whips past, stealing a single black feather.

FOLLOW THE FEATHER, sailing away on the crest of the coming storm: over the mountains, over the trees, sweeping through the canyons where the big trucks strain against the growing gale and turn on their lights in the sudden semi-darkness (though the clocks on their dashboards read straight-up noon). On and on the feather flies, south and east and down and down, over the Santa Susanna Pass, and into the Valley . . .

Where it sticks under the windscreen wiper of an old black pick-up with Texas registration plates, just now pulling up to a little apartment block across from the river.

"Look!" says Pete. "Lucky feather! See it?"

Frankie Miller reaches around and plucks it out, studies it for a moment. "Nice one," he says, handing it to Pete.

"You want it?" Pete asks. "I can find another one."

It takes his dad a while to answer. Pete doesn't blame him. It's a really good feather. "No, thanks," Frankie Miller says firmly. "I'd prob'ly just lose it. You hang on to it for me, okay?"

"Okay," says Pete. "Thanks for the ride." He looks at Ruby. She's sitting there between them with her arms folded. Pete gives her a nudge. He doesn't want their daddy to think they have bad manners. But she doesn't say anything. So he opens the door, and they both climb out.

"You didn't have to be so mean," says Pete, as the truck goes off down the street. "He said he was sorry."

Ruby looks at him like he's crazy. "What good is sorry?" she asks. And then she stomps off into the flat.

Pete sits out on the porch for a while, watching the wind blow leaves and paper and stuff around. He likes it when it blows like this. He wishes they lived someplace where they had hurricanes and all that. Or blizzards. That would be really great. It snowed one time when they lived in Texas; there's a picture of him standing in it, holding Ruby's hand. It's sitting in there on the television right now. 'Course he was just a baby then, so he can't really remember it or anything. He wishes he could remember stuff better.

Rumble, rumble, rumble . . .

Maybe it'll rain really hard, and the river will get all full, like it does in the winter, and Pete'll make a paper boat and put it in there, and it'll sail all the way to the ocean. That's where the river goes. Mama showed him on a map one time. It doesn't seem like much of a river, until you think about that. Or when you get down close to it, like when they're painting the wall. You can see all kinds of stuff then. There's green feathery things growing in there, and sometimes little bitty fishes, and reeds sticking out of some of the cracked-up places. And those long-legged birds that come poking around in there for their supper, picking up their feet real high. And the pigeons, of course. Pete counted sixty-three once. People think it's a tame river, but he knows better. One time he even saw a big old turtle, sitting on a tyre.

He twirls his lucky feather around between his thumb and pointing finger. Why'd Ruby keep saying that wasn't their daddy, anyway? Pete knows it's him. He had pictures of both of 'em on his wall and everything. Pete saw 'em when he went in to go to the toilet. Not very good ones, though. Not like the ones Mama puts all over their flat, with Pete and Ruby right in the middle of the frames, smiling and stuff. These were mostly kind of faraway and fuzzy-looking – just the side of Ruby in one, when she's walking somewhere, and Pete playing ball at break, stuff like that. Looked like they never did hold still for the camera, like Mama always makes 'em. But they couldn't help it; they didn't know their daddy was taking 'em, that was the problem.

It thunders again, and Pete's stomach growls, right at

the same time. *Rumble, rumble, rumble*. What time is it, anyway? He checks his watch: 12.57 p.m. Maybe he better go fix a peanut butter sandwich. He hopes Mama got more blackberry jam. He likes blackberry the best. And the crunchy kind of peanut butter. Last time she got mixed up and bought the wrong kind; it was really terrible. Plus it was the giant size, too; Pete thought they never would get finished with . . .

The front door bangs open. Ruby comes slamming out through it.

"What do they think they're doing?" she asks, pointing across the river.

"Who?" says Pete. And then he sees what she sees: Big Skinny and Mouse, just coming down the access trail to the scaffolding.

"Hey, guys!" Pete hollers, waving, but they don't act like they hear him, with the wind blowing so hard and all. Mouse is leading the way this time. He's got a paint brush and a can of paint in his hands. And Big Skinny is following right behind him and shaking his head and saying something or other – *No, no, no*, is what it looks like from here.

"We aren't supposed to work today, are we?" asks Pete. Doesn't seem like such a great idea now, anyway. It's starting to rain.

"He's changing the eyes again, that's what he's doing," says Ruby. "Sneaking around when he thinks nobody's looking. Do you believe that?" She starts walking over that way – well, more than walking, really. Pete has to run to catch up with her.

"Where you going, Ruby? It's time for lunch."

"Go home, Pete," she calls over her shoulder. "I'll be right back."

But he doesn't want to miss this, whatever it is, and anyway she seems kind of crazy today. Pete figures he better keep an eye on her.

"Go *home*, Pete!"

But he shakes his head, and there's nothing she can do about it because he's seven now. She can't boss him around all the time like she did when he was little. And now they're across the bridge and climbing under the fence (even though it's kind of muddy already) and running over to the scaffolding, and just then there's a flash of lightning, making the sky all bright. *BOOM!* goes the thunder almost right away, so it must be close, not even time to get to two seconds. Seems like it makes the whole scaffolding shake, just when they're climbing on it.

"I don't think this is a very good idea," says Pete. It's starting to rain a little harder now, making splashes on the green water. The rails feel slimy. Pete doesn't much like to touch 'em but he has to because it's slippery up here now. It's dangerous, somebody could fall. But Ruby isn't listening. She's too busy hollering at Mouse.

"What do you think you're doing?"

"Hey, Miller," says Big Skinny. "Hey, champ."

"Hey," says Pete. But Big Skinny isn't really looking at him. He's trying to stand in their path so Ruby can't get to Mouse. Only she's kind of hard to stop when she's mad.

"Get out of my way, Big," she tells him. "I see what he's doing. *I see what you're doing, Mouse!* It's not gonna do you any good, don't you know that? I'm just gonna change 'em back."

But Mouse doesn't say anything, he just keeps slapping that gold paint on the bird eyes, even though it's kind of running a little, on account of the wall, getting wetter all the time.

"I got a lucky feather," Pete says, showing Big Skinny, and he says, "Great," but Pete can tell he's not paying that much attention. And now the rain is starting to *really* come down. "Come on, Ruby," Pete says again, grabbing her arm. "Let's just go eat a sandwich, okay?" But *she's* all slippery too, and when she pulls away – "Let *go* of me, Pete!" – he can't hold on. And now the lightning's flashing all around them and it thunders again – *BOOM!* – and the sky is darker than ever, and Pete hates this whole thing, he really does.

"Come on, Miller," says Big Skinny. He's still trying to hold her back. "Take it easy; it ain't' worth it –"

But he's almost *too* big is the problem, because Ruby just ducks down and scoots under his arm and starts climbing over to where Mouse is. She slips once and falls on her knee, but then she gets up and keeps right on going, even though Mouse won't look at her. He just keeps on painting.

So now Ruby's trying to grab the brush away from him, but he holds it up high and starts throwing it from one hand to another so she can't reach it, and that makes her *really* mad. "You're just wasting your time!" she hollers. "Don't you get it? It's nothing but a fake – it's all a big fat fake – it's nothing but a blue-eyed turkey buzzard!"

Well, shoot, she's talking nuts now. She's starting to scare Pete. "Come on, Ruby," he says as nice as he can, trying to pull on her arm real easy. "Let's go home, okay?" And Big Skinny's trying to get her other arm, but she's too quick. She swings around and shoves him away. And Pete grabs hold of her real tight, because the scaffolding is really shaking this time, and the wind is blowing, and the rain is raining, and there's thunder and lightning all over the place.

"Let *go*, Pete," she yells at him, and she jerks away so hard that he falls back and sort of slips; his foot slips and he's going back and back, and he almost loses his lucky feather, but then he doesn't, he holds on to it after all. And it's a good thing, too, because suddenly there's a weird cracking sound . . .

And now Ruby's face changes, and she's trying to grab hold of *him*, but it's too late, it's all happening too fast; there's nothing behind him but air – *Oh, boy, this is bad, Mama's not gonna like this one bit* – he's just falling and falling and . . .

32

Someone is screaming.

Who's that screaming? Ruby wonders. It sounds like a girl, but there are no girls here but her.

Meanwhile, Pete's lying down there in the shallow green water, half on his back, half on his side.

And he's not moving.

He's not moving, dear God, he's not moving; I've got to get to him . . .

Only her legs are lead; she can barely drag them along.

No! Please no, this isn't happening, no, PETE . . .

And them something . . . two somethings – brush past her, running like the wind. It's Big Skinny and Mouse, miles ahead of her already, running-climbing-jumping down the scaffolding and into the river, getting to Pete in half the time it takes Ruby.

"We've got him! Big Skinny hollers back to her as she struggles towards them. He's kneeling in the water now with Mouse at his side. They've got Pete's head up now; they're pulling him back towards the scaffolding. His eyes are closed – *He's dead*, think Ruby, *Pete's dead, I've killed him* – but now his head moves a little; he's not really awake, but he's coughing, he's spitting out gunk; he's not dead, but there's blood everywhere. Ruby can't tell where it's coming from – his nose mostly, but maybe his ear too, *oh God, oh Pete* . . .

"It's okay, champ," says Big Skinny. "You're all right, buddy, we've got you."

"Pete? Please, Pete . . ." Ruby's there now, trying to take him from the boys. "Can you hear me? It's me, it's Ruby!"

Pete doesn't answer.

Big Skinny shakes his head. "You get up there on the first step, Miller. Me and Mouse'll lift him to you."

But even that little way, Pete groans like it's killing him, though he's not even conscious really; his eyes are still shut tight.

"We shouldn't move him by ourselves. There might be something broken in there," says Big Skinny. "Somebody has to go get help; we gotta call an ambulance."

Ruby shakes her head. She's not going anywhere without Pete.

"I'll go," Mouse mutters.

And just like that he's gone, tearing back up the scaffolding and then who knows where; you can't really see from this far down.

"Will he come back?" Ruby worries.

Big Skinny nods. "He'll come back."

But it seems like for ever and Pete is shivering now; it's freezing all of a sudden. The wind's turned chilly and the rain is pouring down and the river water is cold as ice. Good for woolly mammoths maybe, but not for scrawny little kids. Big Skinny takes off his own T-shirt and tries to wrap it around him, but that's wet too; they're all wet, every inch of them. So Ruby holds him as best she can on one side, and Big Skinny holds him on the other, and they sit there like half-drowned river rats, waiting, in the shadow of the silent giants on the wall. Every one of them – even Mammook – staring through the rain with their sightless eyes, waiting and waiting and waiting . . .

Please, dear God, just let him be all right. I'll do anything. Just don't let him die . . .

And only when Ruby has decided for absolute sure that they'll never see Mouse again, she hears it – like angels singing – the sound of sirens.

Everything that comes next is all a blur, even as it's happening: lights flashing through the downpour, and paramedics bending over Pete, then lowering a stretcher down the scaffolding, somehow, and carrying him away. Ruby tries to follow, but they won't let her, even though she's fighting them, she's fighting them all. But arms keep pulling her back, not just strangers' arms but Big Skinny's and Miss Pierce's and Mouse's, too – he must have gone to her flat to call, Ruby thinks dully somewhere in the back of her brain – and now they're all standing here in the rain saying things to her but none of it makes sense. *Leave me alone, get away, let me stay with my brother!* she yells, but no on pays any attention. *What's this in his hand?* she hears somebody ask. *It's his lucky feather*, she tries to tell them. Somehow all this time, even out cold, he's never let go of it. But they're not listening. They prise his fingers loose so they can put some kind of tube in his wrist, and then they throw the feather on the ground. *It's okay, I'll get it,* says Big Skinny when Ruby cries out, and he picks it up and gives it to her and she runs after the stretcher, but she's too late. They're loading Pete into the ambulance now; they're just closing the door . . .

And suddenly Ed's car is screeching down the access path and Mama is climbing out before it's even stopped all the way. *Where's my baby, what's happening, get out of my WAY!* she's yelling at some guy in a yellow rain cape who's accidentally blocking her path. But it works, at least for Mama. For her they open up: *It's the mother, it's okay, she can go with him.* And then they let her in by the stretcher and slam the door again, and now the siren is wailing like before and the ambulance is racing away, and Ruby breaks from the arms holding her and runs after it: *Take me with you!* she's yelling, but they don't listen, nobody listens . . .

And then a hand catches her shoulder again. "It's okay, Ruby. Come with me, honey. I'll take you; we'll follow them."

And she turns around and sees Ed, with rain running down his face and his half-bald head shining red — on again, off again — as the police-car lights turn round and round. Good old Ed, solid as a rock, all eighty man-eating-chicken kilos of him. So Ruby nods and starts running to the car . . .

"Just a minute," says one of the policemen, "we have a few questions."

Oh, please, thinks Ruby, *please no, not now, we don't have TIME to be arrested again* . . . But Ed takes the cop aside and gives him some kind of card and says something to him; Ruby can't hear what it is but it must be good — it works, anyway — because the policeman nods, finally, and steps aside, and they all breathe a sigh of relief and start piling in Ed's car (all but Mouse, that is, whose dad appears out of nowhere, cursing and steaming. "Call me!" Mouse hollers as he's being dragged away). And now they're racing through the rain-slick streets, with the police car going ahead of them, flashing its lights and blasting its siren, all the way to the hospital.

But they won't let Ruby see Pete here either. They stick her and Big Skinny in some stupid waiting room, while Ed and Miss Pierce go off to find out whatever they can.

"Let me go with you," Ruby begs, but Ed says it's better if she stays here; they can probably get further without her.

"I'll come back the second I know anything. I promise."

"Okay," she says after a moment. She doesn't know him all that well, really (even if he *has* been around every day all summer long), but she knows she can believe him. She knows that much. "Give him his lucky feather," she says, handing it over. She looks at Miss Pierce. "It's important."

So the old folks nod and go off towards the lifts, and

now it's just the two of them, Ruby and Big Skinny (well, them and a few dozen others), crammed up next to a fake-wood table piled with dog-eared copies of month-old magazines – The World's Sexiest Man issue of *People* and a *Newsweek* with the Pope on the cover and something called *Fit Over Fifty*, with a tough-looking old guy lifting weights under the large-print headline: IF WAYNE CAN DO IT, SO CAN YOU . . .

Seems like they sit there for a long, long time.

"You okay?" Big Skinny asks after a while.

Ruby looks up. She'd almost forgotten he was here. He looks strange. Why does he look like that? Her brain can't put it all together. It's the jacket, that's what it is; he's wearing Ed's Chiropody Centre anorak . . . Why is he wearing that?

Then she remembers . . . Big Skinny's T-shirt, red with Pete's blood, wrapped around Pete's bony little shoulders.

Her eyes have been dry as sandpaper all this time, but now she covers her mouth with both hands, trying to stop the sob that wants to escape.

"Aw, Miller, don't cry. Please don't cry." He puts an arm around her. She tries to pull away, but he won't let her; he sticks like glue. "He's gonna be okay. He's tough, you know? He's the champ. He's gonna be fine."

"It was my fault," says Ruby. She doesn't mean to say it. The words come out of her mouth before she knows they're coming.

"No, it wasn't; it wasn't anybody's fault. It was an accident, that's all."

"I just . . . I didn't want Mouse to change the stupid *eyes*, can you believe that? I mean, what did it matter what colour they were? Why'd I even care?"

"Well, that's okay, Miller; you just wanted it to look good, that's all. That's what I tried to tell Mouse, but you know how he is. You and him's both the same type of perfectionists, I guess."

"By why did *he* care? It's all so stupid . . ."

"Well, he just couldn't stand for it to be wrong, that's all. He said he shouldn't have got it wrong in the first place, but he did the little picture in kind of a hurry, you see. We didn't have much time, so he was just guessing about the eyes, but then later on he checked it out, just to make sure."

"What do you mean? What little picture?"

"Well, you know, the Ice Age picture. You remember – the one we gave Pete for his birthday."

"The birthday picture?" Suddenly Ruby feels dizzy. "With – with Mammook and the sabre-toothed tigers and – and – *Mouse* painted that?"

"Aw, man." Big Skinny shakes his head. "I'm sorry, I guess I wasn't really supposed to tell. He's been kind of getting a kick out being anonymous. You know, so it would be almost like magic, like Santa Claus or somebody."

"It was *Mouse's* idea?"

"Well, we all sort of thought of it together, I guess. After Pete said he wanted a time machine. Old Ed, he made the frame; plus it was him who told us the whole story about the puppet and all. And Miss Pierce even helped out some. She hid it over at her flat till it was time. But Mouse — well, you've seen his art stuff in the hall at school — the Creature from the Black Lagoon, remember? You know, the one on the motorcycle? Nobody can paint like Mouse."

The Lizard Guy — that was *his*? Mouse is an *artist*? She'd forgotten — if she ever knew in the first place. Until they got stuck together with the Duke of Wellington, Ruby never gave Matthew Mossbach a second thought.

Big Skinny sighs. "I'm sorry, Miller, I just figured you knew. I thought for sure your mother would've said something, or . . . well, shoot, who'd you *think* painted it?"

Ruby stares at her hands. They're so dirty, you could practically plant grass. But what does it matter now? What did it ever matter? It's all so stupid. "I thought it was my dad," she says.

"Oh." Big Skinny is quiet for a moment. "Well, sure you did — that makes sense. I'm sorry, Miller. I'm awful sorry."

You'll never know how sorry . . .

I was afraid I'd mess it up again . . .

What good is sorry?

Let GO, Pete . . .

"It's not your fault," she says. She wishes it was. She wishes she could blame somebody else, *anybody* else. But it wasn't Big Skinny who pushed Pete away. It wasn't him standing there like an ice sculpture when Pete hit the water. Oh, no, it was Ruby, from first to last, her and her all-electric ideas . . .

She stares out of the waiting-room window. It's still pouring outside. She can see a long ribbon of headlights snaking through the gloom, a never-ending line of indignant Southern Californians, honking and skidding along the slippery boulevard. A million cars, with a million drivers, not one of them worrying about the little kid with the freckles and the calibrated sports watch. He could disappear without a trace, and they'd never know the difference. They'd go on asking for fries with their hamburgers just the same. But it wasn't their fault, either. They weren't the sorry ones.

"Ruby?"

It's Ed with Miss Pierce, back from their search. Ruby was staring so hard out of the window, she didn't see them coming. But now she jumps up –

"Did you see him? What'd they say? He's not . . . Pete's not . . . ."

Ed puts a hand on her shoulder. "He's going to be all right, honey. He's got concussion, they think, and a couple of bones broken in one arm. And some nasty bruises, of course, but –"

She doesn't wait for him to finish. She throws her arms around his waist, hangs on for dear life. "Are you sure? You're sure? Can I see him now?"

"You can see him. Just for a little while; he's pretty much out of it. But the doctor said you could both go in for a few minutes. They've just put him in room three twenty-four."

"Okay, come on, Big. Let's go."

"No, Vincent, you stay with us. Just immediate family right now."

Ruby doesn't understand. Didn't he say "both"? Well, never mind; room 324 – she'll have to take the lift, right? "Is that up or down or –"

And then she sees him standing in the doorway a few feet behind Ed. Just standing there, waiting, with his baseball cap in his hands.

Miss Pierce follows her eyes. "Your mother called him," she says.

Oh. Right. He's in the phone book, remember?

Big Skinny looks worried. "You okay, Miller?"

Ruby nods. She takes a deep breath. "Three twenty-four?"

"Three twenty-four," says Ed.

They don't talk much in the lift. Or in the corridor either.

The soles of their shoes make more noise, squeaking along the linoleum, than either of the people wearing them.

"Come in," Mama says quietly, when Frankie taps on the door.

And there's Pete in the big hospital bed, looking like he's dressed up for Hallowe'en – like one of his mummies, from the shoulders up. But it's Pete, no question about it, even with tubes coming out of him every which way, and his arm trussed up like a turkey. You can see the red curls sticking out the top of the bandage on his head.

"Hello, Frankie," says Mama.

"Hey, Pearl." He hangs back at the door, holding on to that old cap.

But Ruby runs straight to her mother.

"Oh, Mama." She's in her arms now. "I'm sorry. I'm so sorry . . ."

"I know, baby."

"Is he really okay? Are you sure?"

"He'll be fine. Just fine." She looks at Frankie. "He said it was a good thing he had his lucky feather."

They're all quiet for a moment, thinking that over. Then Mama leans in closer to the bed, touches the freckled cheek with the back of her hand. "Pete? Pete, honey, they're here."

"Don't wake him," says Frankie. "He needs his rest."

"It's all right. He wants to see you. He's been asking for you. Pete?"

Pete's eyes open. They might be the twin blue mirrors of Frankie's, looking back at him. He smiles. "Hey, Daddy." He sounds kind of strange. His tongue must be feeling a little thick from the painkillers or something.

"Hello, son."

Pete looks at Ruby. "I told you it was him."

"I know. I was wrong. I'm sorry, Pete."

Frankie clears his throat. "How you feeling there, partner?"

"Okay."

"Anything I can get you? Y'all need any – any ice or anything?"

Mama shakes her head. "We're all right."

"Well, that's good." Frankie nods. "That's real good." He folds his cap in two, tucks the brim in, flips it out again. Reaches for the doorknob. "Well, I guess . . . I guess I ought to let you get some rest now, right? But if . . . well, if you think of anything, just –"

Pete mutters something. It's getting harder to understand him. He tugs on Ruby's arm with his unhurt hand.

"What?" Ruby leans in. "What'd you say, Pete?"

Pete scrunches up his eyebrows, tries again. "You still got his yo-yo?"

His yo-yo? "I don't know . . " Ruby'd forgotten all about it. Seems like a million years since she put it in her pocket this morning. But it's there, all right. Just a little damp from the rain and the river. She walks across the room, gives it to Frankie. "I guess he wants to know if you can still do your tricks."

Frankie stands there for a second, turning it over. He looks at Mama. She nods. He pauses again. Starts to put his cap back on. Changes his mind, puts it on a chair. Then he slips the loop of the grimy old string around his finger, gives the yo-yo a couple of flicks of the wrist . . .

He's kind of rusty. You can see he's out of practice. But he gets the hang of it again pretty quick. Walk the Dog, that's no trouble at all; and Rock the Cradle . . .

he's finding his rhythm now. And when that little blue Man on the Flying Trapeze spins through the air, and lands on the string, and then bounces back up and twirls around *again* . . .

Frankie's children are both smiling.

"More," says Pete.

33

CUT TO: The river.

Dedication Day, two weeks later.

The storm is long gone. It blew on south and east into Mexico finally, even touching the tail end of Texas with a squall or two, but not before snarling up traffic on the main highway for twenty-four hours straight, breaking every record for August rainfall in the history of the Valley, and raising the entire Los Angeles River several sparkling inches.

"What do you figure now?" Big Skinny asks Mouse. "Couple of feet?" The two of them are sitting just to Ruby's left on the portable benches the Friends have set up on Valleyheart Drive. They're facing the mighty mural, which you can't really see just yet. The scaffolding is gone, along with every last paint can and roller brush, but an enormous red, white and blue tarpaulin is draped over the wall now, waiting for the unveiling ceremonies to begin.

"Naw, a foot, tops," says Mouse. "But at least it

smells better." He pokes Big Skinny in the ribs. "Least until the stink bomb goes off, right, Big?"

Ruby's heart sinks. Good grief. "You're kidding, right? You better be kidding."

"I'm kidding, I'm kidding . . ."

"He's kidding . . ."

Thank God. And it does smell better, come to think of it. The whole world smells better. Ruby breathes in the clean air, the whole shining afternoon. It might be the first week of June, not September, and summer just starting, not ending. She looks across the river. Pete's pigeons are raising their wings for another round. The show must be about to begin.

Lucky thing, too. The crowd is getting restless; the benches are nearly full already. She never did get around to inviting Mr Spielberg after all, but it looks like just about everybody else is here: the Mayor and a boatload of politicians and the alien truck driver and all the other Friends and volunteers and sour-faced Theo and Detective Donner and Mrs Haines and Charlotte Burton and most everybody from school and a hundred little kids with balloons tied to their wrists, not to mention a half-dozen clowns from Pagliacci's, every one of them rented and paid for by David R. Davis, who it turns out might just be the richest Gatekeeper on this planet or any other. He's sitting in the front row, a few feet below Ruby, with Thelma on a purple-sequinned leash at his side. Looks like she's covering the other guy next to her (good grief, is that the Moustache Man?) with her slobberiest kisses.

And of course Miss Pierce is down there at the podium with Lord Byron, checking out the public address system. "Testing, testing, one, two, three . . ."

"Shut up, baby," says the bird.

Ruby laughs with everybody else, but she's glad *she* doesn't have to be the one to stand up in front of all these people and say inspiring things. She's perfectly happy to be sitting here with the guys on her left, and Pete on her right – he's got just one black eye now, and a cast on his arm so covered with doodles and autographs, you can hardly see the plaster – and Mama beside him, with her new ring sparkling on her finger, and Ed beside Mama, visiting with Big Skinny's grandmother, who's sitting on *his* right . . .

"Ah, *buon giorno*!" she says to Ruby, when they're introduced. "*Molta bella!* With the red hair! *L'amore dei Vincente, no?*"

"*Buon giorno*," says Ruby, blushing clear up to those very red roots. "Just a friend, that's all."

Big Skinny is blushing too. "She's a little hard of hearing. Sometimes she gets things kind of mixed up."

"It's okay," says Ruby. "I think it's nice, the way she says your name."

"You do?" Big Skinny looks like he might pass out on the spot. "Well, maybe if you want to, you could call me Vincente."

Ruby thinks that over. "Okay." She scrapes a drop of bird-poo off the bench. "And maybe you could call me Ruby."

"Okay." Big Skinny grins hugely. Ruby tries not to

groan. (He did save her brother's life, after all.) He gives Mouse a nudge.

Mouse rolls his eyes. "Maybe you could kiss my rosy red —"

"Watch it, Mouse!"

"I'm kidding! I'm kidding! Can't anybody take a joke around here?" Mouse sighs. "Call me Matthew, if you feel like it."

"Testing, testing, one, two, three . . ."

Miss Pierce is clearing her throat now. The crowd starts quietening down a bit. *Oh, boy, this is really it then. But where is . . .*

Ruby looks around. You can't see much of anything, with all these people. Probably the parking was terrible; there's no telling how far he had to walk. Or he might have had a flat tyre, or —

"Excuse me . . . sorry . . . Didn't mean to step on you there, sir . . ."

And then she spots him, climbing up from the bottom row, where he's stopped to speak to Thelma and Mr Davis.

"Sorry," he says again, scooting into the place Ruby and Pete are making between them. "Am I late?"

"No, she's only getting started," says Ruby. "You're just in time."

Miss Pierce clears her throat once more:

> "*So may you paint your picture, twice show truth,*
> *Beyond mere imagery on the wall, —*
> *So, note by note, bring music from your mind,*

> *Deeper than ever e'en Beethoven dived, —*
> *So write a book shall mean beyond the facts,*
> *Suffice the eye and save the soul beside."*

Every cell in Ruby's body is tingling. Man, if she could just write like *that* . . . She looks in her programme for the author. Some guy named Robert Browning. She wonders if he's written any screenplays. Maybe she should check it out.

And save the soul beside . . . Beside what? Ruby wonders. She doesn't understand it, not really. But maybe that doesn't matter so much. Maybe some words just *are*, like oxygen.

And now the Rutherford B. Hayes Middle School band starts playing . . . *O beautiful for spacious skies* . . . and the workers start pulling the ropes, and the star-spangled tarpaulin is raised, and a gasp goes around the crowd. Or not a gasp exactly, this time, more of an *Ohhhhhhhhh* . . . And then everybody starts clapping and whistling . . .

And it's wonderful, it really is. It's kind of amazing, when you think about it. They *did* that, didn't they? Only . . .

"I thought it would turn out better," says Mouse. He and Ruby and Big Skinny and Pete are still sitting in the bleachers, staring, after most of the crowd has gone.

"No," says Ruby. "It's really good, Mou — Matthew."

"Are you kidding me?" Big Skinny slaps him on the back. "It's *great*!"

"You really think so?"

"Absolutely."

"No question about it."

"It's perfect," says Pete, looking right at Mouse.

Good grief. He doesn't KNOW, does he? No way; he's just seven years old. He couldn't POSSIBLY have known all along . . .

Could he?

"Thanks," says Mouse. Seems like that does make him feel a little better, even if he doesn't appear entirely convinced.

And Ruby wouldn't say it aloud, not in a trillion years, but the truth is — well, it's *not* perfect, really. It's *not* what she saw in her mind that day on the porch, that golden glorious vision she's been dreaming of all this time.

Not exactly.

But you know what?

It's not too bad.

MOVE IN CLOSE on the mighty painted condor, its giant wings outspread, frozen in flight high above the painted river. Closer . . . still closer . . . As the camera ZOOMS IN on the brush strokes of the great bird's golden eye, a shadow passes across it, making it appear – for just a fraction of a second – almost as it –

No, wait!!! Good heavens!!! This is no illusion!!! That bird just BLINKED, no question about it!!! He's turning his head; he's beating his wings; he's breaking free from his concrete bonds. And now, all around him and beneath him, the rest of the painting is coming to life, too: huge, chunks of plaster fall away from the river wall and CRASH into the clamorous current. Swordfish leap, giant sloths nibble on treetops, mammoths move with a ponderous (yet prudent) grace, ever wary of the dire wolves, the sinister sabre-toothed cats, prowling all too lean and hungrily at the water's edge.

And yet . . . and yet . . . in their untamed midst, a stunning young woman (fair WINONA, THE WARRIOR PRINCESS) waits calmly, fearlessly, beside the raucous roar of the rapids. Suddenly the gallant condor sweeps low before her. They know each other at once. With a joyful cry, he bears her skyward on his mighty wings . . .

"Ruby? Pete? Come on, you guys! We can catch the twilight show if we hurry!"

Ruby comes back down from the clouds. "Be right there!"

Mr Spielberg will just have to wait. Her daddy's taking her to see a film, and she doesn't want to miss a single minute.

She's crazy about beginnings.

MANY THANKS TO:

Ed Formosa, artist extraordinaire

The Salvation Army, especially Kirk, Jared and Mark (Van Nuys, California), and Josh (Woodland Hills, California)

George C. Page Museum of La Brea Discoveries, Los Angeles

Judith F. Baca and everyone at SPARC: The Social and Public Art Resource Centre, Venice, California

The Sespe Condor Sanctuary, Fillmore, California

The Friends of the Los Angeles River

Wade Graham, author of "This Way, L.A.", *Los Angeles Times Magazine,* December 3, 2000

David Ferrell, author of "L.A. River Defies City in Nurturing Wildlife", *Los Angeles Times*, July 26, 2001

David Walter Cooney and all his children of the heart, especially Steven A.

William Joseph Nelson Jr and his parents, Ginger and William Nelson Sr

Susannah, Peter and Clare Fields Flood

Charles and Chesley Krohn

David Doty

Carlin Glynn and Peter Masterson

William Goldman

Linda Crew

Amy and Sy Kellman

Dr William McKee of the University of St Thomas, Houston, Texas

Turner Classic Movies, courtesy of Claire and Tom McLaurin

Frances Elliot

David and Carroll Nelson

Will and Patsy Mackenzie

Judie Angell and Phil Gaberman

Sheila Tybor, master teacher, and her former student Everett Robinson

Adam Jackson, who actually understands computers

Virginia Skrelja, Ginee Seo, Jeannie Ng and everyone at Simon & Schuster Children's Publishing

Dick Jackson, always and for ever

AND MOST ESPECIALLY TO:

Kevin Cooney, lunatic genius, and our children, Michael, Errol, Gina and Brian Cooney

- with all my love, and apologies to Pooh